PENGUIN BOOKS

12 EDMONDSTONE STREET

David Malouf was born in Brisbane. His father's family came to Australia in the 1880s from Lebanon and his mother's family from London just before the First World War. He was educated at the Brisbane Grammar School and the University of Queensland, where he taught for two years after completing a degree. At the age of twenty-four he left Australia and remained abroad for nearly ten years, teaching in England and travelling in Europe. In 1968 he returned to Australia and was appointed senior tutor and later lecturer at Sydney University. He now lives in Italy.

David Malouf's most recent novel, *Harland's Half Acre*, was published in 1984 (Penguin 1985). His many awards include the N.S.W. Premier's Award for Fiction for *An Imaginary Life*, the 1982 Melbourne *Age* Book of the Year Award for *Fly Away Peter* (Penguin 1983), and the Australian Literature Society's Gold Medal in 1974 for *Neighbours in a Thicket*, a collection of poems, and in 1983 for *Fly Away Peter*. In 1985 a collection of his short stories appeared under the title *Antipodes* (Penguin 1986) and in the same year he was awarded the Vance Palmer Award for Fiction.

DAVID MALOUF

12 Edmondstone Street

PENGUIN BOOKS

Penguin Books Ltd, Harmondsworth, Middlesex, England
Viking Penguin Inc., 40 West 23rd Street, New York, New York 10010, U.S.A.
Penguin Books Australia Ltd, Ringwood, Victoria, Australia
Penguin Books Canada Limited, 2801 John Street, Markham, Ontario,
Canada L3R 1B4
Penguin Books (N.Z.) Ltd, 182–190 Wairau Road, Auckland 10, New Zealand

First published by Chatto & Windus · The Hogarth Press 1985
Published in Penguin Books 1986

'A Place in Tuscany' and 'A Foot in the Stream'
were originally published in the *National Times*.

Printed and bound in Great Britain by
Cox & Wyman Ltd, Reading
Typeset in Palatino

CONTENTS

For my sister, Jill

12 Edmondstone Street

[1]

Memory plays strange tricks on us. The house I lived in as a child is no longer there. Like most of old South Brisbane it has been torn down and a factory stands on the site, part of a process that had already begun when I first knew the area more than forty years ago.

Edmondstone Street even then was 'mixed'. Beginning at Melbourne Street, not far from the Bridge, and skirting the south side of Musgrave Park – a dark, uneven place, once an aboriginal burial ground but later redeemed and laid out with Moreton Bay figs of enormous girth and a twelve-foot checker-board – it consisted chiefly of old-fashioned, many-roomed houses from the days when this was the most fashionable area south of the river; but there were factories as well, Simpson's Flour and the Vulcan Can Company, and a private hospital, the Yasmar, so called because it was the matron's name spelt backwards. I was born there, so was my sister; and in due course, after the fashion of those times, we went back and had our tonsils removed.

The Yasmar was pulled down in the sixties, along with two houses, the grandest in the street, where I had sometimes gone in the afternoons to play. They were houses like our own, but belonged to families who were better off than we were and could keep them up. One of them had a tennis court that was still mowed and rolled every Wednesday afternoon, with a formal garden and orchard beyond. Only the sag-ging wire fence of our tennis court survived. Behind it my grandfather had a vegetable patch and a dozen noisy chooks.

Nothing much remains of Edmondstone Street, and our house, Number twelve, went ages ago, though I recall it well enough; I can feel my way in the dark through every room. The trick of memory I refer to has nothing to do with that. It concerns the work my father did on the house towards the end of the war.

12 Edmondstone Street was a one-storeyed weatherboard, a style of house so common then as to be quite unremarkable; Brisbane was a one-storeyed weatherboard town. It stood on low stilts at the front, high stilts at the back, and was essentially a nest of open rooms surrounded on three sides by wide, cooling verandahs, ironwork to the rails, in a pattern of interlocking circles, and rolled venetians above. The ironwork was cream, the venetians ochre, the square wooden supports with their branches and volutes a spanking white, and the roof, which was of iron, that dull ox-blood colour that is so peculiar to Brisbane that it seems more dominant even, in the long view, than the green of the enormous shade-trees – mangoes, hoop-pines, all the varieties of subtropical fig – that darken every backyard.

South Brisbane then was already disreputable, too close to the derelict, half-criminal life of Stanley Street where the abos were and to Musgrave Park with its swaggies and metho-drinkers.

When they first came to Brisbane in the 1880s my grandparents lived in Stanley Street, in one room below street level. My father remembered the place and spoke of how they had been driven out of it in the '93 flood, when all the south side of the river was under water; but this must have been a memory by hearsay; he wasn't born until 1896. Later the family moved to a shop at the corner of Melbourne and Edmondstone Streets, a big general store and milk bar with high ceilings made of beaten tin, electric fans, soda fountains and several marble-topped tables on wrought-iron feet.

One of these tables, in the corner by the door, was my grandfather's. When he was not working in our back yard, turning a bit of suburban South Brisbane into a Mediterranean garden, he would hold court there; and I use the phrase 'hold court' not as an empty metaphor but to suggest the dignity with which he waited for his adherents to appear, and the kindly condescension with which they were received: people from the community who were seeking advice or asking for letters to be written to the Old Country; others, old men like himself, very formal in collarless shirts and suits, who wanted to hear a story told by someone who was educated in their language and skilled in the art of narration. The stories were like poems, full of repeated figures and odd rhetorical questions to which the listeners sometimes, like children, would call out the answer and then shyly laugh. They all knew the stories by heart but only he had the skill, or the right, to tell them. Listening at the edge of the circle, with my chin resting on the bent cane back of a chair, I would get so lost in the telling that I almost understood: not the words but the tune. Though it was really my grandfather who interested me, and he remained unknowable since I could not speak to him; close, even companionable when he called me to help him dig, but a mystery.

Sometimes unshaven, often collarless, but always in a three-piece suit with watch chain and walking stick, he had a dignity that was disproportionate here; disproportionate as well to the shop and its suburban comings and goings. Unless you thought of him as the exiled ruler of a minor kingdom still receiving courtiers in a far-off place. Or unless you knew, as I did, the portrait of his brother the Bishop, which hung in my grandmother's sitting-room among the buttoned-leather chairs. It had been presented to the family when that prince of the church, a Rasputin-like figure, long-bearded, black-gowned, with a high oriental hat and a pectoral cross, had made a visit to Australian Maronites in the early Twenties. The image was hieratic. You saw that immediately. So was my grandfather's when he sat at his corner table drinking tea from a glass and wetting his drooping moustache, or when he leaned on the handle of his stick and considered a move on the cribbage-board. Very mild and familiar, it was hard to believe he had known a place where whole villages could be wiped out in a single afternoon. The shop was such a backwater. Our own afternoons, so warm and still, seemed far from even the echo of violence. And the language in which he and his cronies went over it all, the fearful history, the litany of names, the village jests and insults, was so softly guttural and cooing.

Meanwhile my aunts, his three unmarried daughters, would be dealing with grubby message lists in the hands of toddlers, weighing out lollies in little white packets, scooping ice cream from frosted tubs; or to the old man's infinite disgust, entertaining nuns in the downstairs kitchen. He didn't care for nuns, and these were from St Mary's. Irish. His girls had abandoned the Maronite church for the local Catholic one. The saints they invoked he had never caught breath of in the Old Country. He stuck to his old men and his tales from the Arabian Nights.

My father too had betrayed him; or had, in his quiet way, adapted himself so completely to this new place that there was no link between them. But then, my father was born here, had grown up 'Australian' in the rough South Brisbane 'pushes' before the Great War: a clean-cut Catholic boy working for the St Vincent de Paul on Saturday mornings, playing League on Saturday afternoons, and on weekdays driving his own horse and dray – which would later become a truck, then a whole fleet of them.

My father had had to leave school at twelve. He was the only support of his mother and six children. What, I wonder now, was his relationship with the old man (who can't have been old then) whose temperament, or aristocratic pride, or lack of English, or contempt for the conventions of the place, made it impossible for him to take employment, but who saw nothing shameful in having his wife drudge sixteen hours a day in a shop, and his children, one after the other, go to work as my father did, selling newspapers at tram stops, running messages for people, saving up to buy the horse and dray. My father, I think, was too dutiful, too deeply imbued, for all his Australianness, with Old Country notions of filial piety, to be critical of his father – though I can't speak for his feelings. He never expressed them. He didn't show them either. When he married he bought a house two doors from his mother's (he was, by then, thirty-eight), and my grandmother, a small, fine-boned, demanding woman, was a heavy presence in our house, though she never in fact entered it. She sent her daughters up each Friday, in the early years of my parents' marriage, to see that the 'girl', Mrs Hall or Nan or Reenie or whoever it happened to be, was frying fish in oil rather than fat and that there was no meat in the house. My mother lost several good housekeepers in this way till we got Cassie. Cassie could stand up for herself, and being Catholic, unlike the others, was aware at least of the rudiments of the faith.

My father had never strayed far from where he started – that arc of the river between the city reach at Victoria Bridge and the West End reach at Davies Park. Our house was at the very centre of it, a low part of town in every sense, which is why immigrants settled there, and why abos, swaggies and metho-drinkers were about. When Brisbane became a garrison town in 1942, the jumping-off point for General Douglas MacArthur's Pacific campaign, the city was segregated to propitiate American fears of race riots, and the South Side, our side, was declared black. Our grand house, which had always been on shaky ground, became an island of light in the general blackout and we were forbidden to play outside the yard. More and more it was a little world of its own, to be mapped, explored, re-mapped, interpreted and made the repository of its own powerful mythology.

First houses are the grounds of our first experience. Crawling about at floor level, room by room, we discover laws that we will apply later to the world at large; and who is to say if our notions of space and dimension are not determined for all time by what we encounter there, in the particular relationship of living-rooms to attic and cellar (or in my case under-the-house), of inner rooms to the verandahs that are open boundaries?

Each house has its own topography, its own lore: negotiable borders, spaces open or closed, the salient features – not Capes and Bays in this case but the Side Door, the Brass Jardinière – whose names make up a daily litany. A complex history comes down to us, through household jokes and anecdotes, odd habits, irrational superstitions. Its spirit resides in ordinary objects that become, beyond the fact of presence and usefulness, the characters in a private language – characters too in the story we are living. We hear our first folk tales with a start of recognition, since what is enacted in them is general to every society, even the smallest, and our own has already revealed to us the magic that glows along a threshold or round a forbidden biscuit tin. The house is a field of dense affinities, laid down, each one, with an almost physical power, in the life we share with all that in being 'familiar' has become essential to us, inseparable from what we are. We are drawn back magically, magnetically, to our own sticky fingerprints. Even in their ghostly state, on objects long since dispersed. They haunt us. Set loose in a world of *things*, we are struck at first by their terrible otherness. It drives us to fury. For a time, while we are all mouth, we try to swallow them, then to smash them to smithereens – little hunters on the track of the ungraspable. Till we perceive at last that in naming and handling things we have power over them. If they refuse to yield their history to us they may at least, in time, become agents in ours. This is the process of our first and deepest education. A 'secret machinery' gets to work in us, 'a hidden industry of the senses and the spirit' whose busy handling and hearing and overhearing is our second birth into the world – into that peculiar embodiment of it that is a household and a house.

But 12 Edmondstone Street as I remember it was really two houses: an earlier one, almost unchanged from the beginning of the century, and a later one as it was 'done up' during the war.

Like most people in those days, my father was ashamed of our house. He would have preferred a modern one made of brick. Weatherboard was too close to beginnings, to a dependence on what was merely local and near to hand rather than expensively imported. It was native, provincial, poverty-stricken – poor white. Real cities, as everyone knows, are made to last. They have foundations set firm in the earth. Weatherboard cities float above it on blocks or stumps. Weatherboard houses can be lifted if necessary, loaded on to the back of a lorry and set down again two suburbs or a thousand miles away. They have about them the improvised air of tree houses. Airy, open, often with no doors between the rooms, they are on such easy terms with breezes, with the thick foliage they break into at window level, with the lives of possums and flying-foxes, that living in them, barefoot for the most part, is like living in a reorganised forest. The creak of timber as the day's heat seeps away, the gradual adjustment in all its parts, like a giant instrument being tuned, of the house-frame on its stumps, is a condition of life that goes deep into consciousness. It makes the timberhouse-dweller, among the domesticated, a distinct subspecies, somewhere between bushie and brick-and-mortar man.

As for verandahs. Well, their evocation of the raised tent flap gives the game away completely. They are a formal confession that you are just one step up from nomads.

As soon as it was possible under the building restrictions, a weatherboard house, if it was not to be demolished altogether, should be closed in; and so it was, late in the war, that my father ripped out our verandah lace, dismantled the venetians and, after 'boarding in' to rail height, installed louvres in galvanised frames. At the same time the house was divided into flats. My sister and I got a bedroom at last on the side verandah, our spare room became a dining-room kitchen, and newly weds (a nice quiet couple in their forties) moved into the rooms at the back. The one surviving room from what had been the coolest, closest, most lived-in part of our house was the bathroom, but we entered it now from the other side.

And here I come at last to that trick of memory with which I began. The fact is that however hard I try, I cannot find this new door or remember where it was. I know where it ought to be, but when I shut my eyes I can't see it; and though I must, in the years after the house was changed, have gone through it a thousand times, I cannot, in memory, set my hand to the doorknob or put my body in the frame. I still enter by the earlier door, one step up from the kitchen on the other side.

Impossible, of course. But I hang on hard to this failure of memory, this impossibility, because it allows me, almost by accident, to keep my larger memory whole. So long as that door remains blank, and our handyman, Old Jack, has not yet taken his hammer to the wall, I can keep our first house undivided, as it was in my earliest experience of it, when I was not yet eight years old; and it is this whole house I want to go back to and explore, rediscovering, room by room, what it was that I first learned there about how high, how wide the world is, how one space opens into another, and from the objects those rooms contained, and the habits and uses they were caught up in (including the forbidden ones), what kind of reality I had been born into, that body of myths, beliefs, loyalties, anxieties, affections that shapes a life, and whose outline we enter and outgrow.

[II]

You approach it from the street via a set of concrete steps. Stained ox-blood red, they rise between grass slopes, no more than twelve feet wide from verandah stump to low street wall, green from constant sprinkling and perfectly trimmed at the edge. The wall has pillars topped with painted spheres and linked with chains that passing larrikins are inclined to swing, though we, obediently, do not.

The verandah door is of lattice, brilliantly white. It is closed but not locked. Inside, three squatter's chairs with extended arms and striped canvas seats stand on one side of it, with a wickerwork chaise, known as the Cane Lounge, on the other. When ladies come to morning or afternoon tea my mother wheels a traymobile out of the Front Room, draws all the chairs together, wrestles with the chains of the venetians, and the Front Verandah becomes a tolerably comfortable place of entertainment; cooler, lighter, certainly airier than the Front Room itself. I cannot imagine circumstances under which daytime visitors would be taken there. Visitors are entertained on the verandah and family and close friends in the kitchen.

The Front Verandah is the place as well where travellers appear and show their wares, men who go from door to door (or did then) with sample-cases containing sheets, towels, pillow-slips, 'longeray' and lines of wholesale grocery. I remember one or two of these fellows for their loud suits and moustaches and their jokey good-humour, or because they would try to ingratiate themselves with the little master of the house by shaking out a stick of Wrigley's chewing-gum, which I regularly, of course, refused. But when I summon up the Front Verandah, my mother's ladies refuse, individually, to appear; they fade into one another in a single hum. Only as I recall them from later occasions, and in other places, do they settle out and become unique characters and stories:

Mrs Robbie, my Aunt Frances's inseparable friend, inseparable herself from a huge clasp handbag in which she appears to be carrying all her household possessions.

The cast of Mrs Robbie's face is downward, as if she were under the influence of an exceptional response to the forces of gravity; or perhaps it is just the burden of her life with 'Robbie'. Her cheeks sag; she has heavy bags under her beadlike eyes, and above them a drooping fold instead of a lid. Her ear lobes are elongated under the weight of antique earrings. Her clothes, which are in tones of brown, are at least two decades out of date. They are composed entirely of tattered shawls and she wears what I see as a string of mothballs round her neck.

Mrs Lewis, who talks – once *she* gets going you can't get a word in edgeways. She's a real ear-basher. Mrs Lewis likes to knit while she talks, and I am fascinated by the correspondence between the endless clatter of her needles and her false teeth, which she appears to have synchronised to the one rhythm. Most ladies use two needles; Mrs Lewis needs three. One purl, one plain, the needles go, but fast – *clackclackclack*. 'I said,' 'she said,' says Mrs Lewis, producing woolly rigmaroles.

Maisie – minxlike. No longer quite young, she has modelled herself on Mrs Simpson. Slim, spruce, tanned, she wears neat little suits with flashes on the lapels, white collars, false bow-ties in pillar-box red and navy, and she paints her legs rather than wear stockings, though you can hardly tell. She is full of quick come-backs and has been something in vaudeville. She knows the show people who appear weekly at the Cremorne, and has the air, still, of being able to tap up a storm or be sawn in two, if required, by a gentleman in tails. She is a tough nut and has once, no doubt, been fast, but she has slowed down in my mother's company and is lady enough in our house never to light up.

But all this is as I come to know them later. Early on they are indistinguishable, just visitors. If, from my end of the verandah, I glance up from playing with one of my toy cars, they are a cloud of whispers and talc, barely held down, they are so volatile, by their earrings, the clasps on their handbags, their bones, the bones in their corsets, their engagement- and wedding-rings, and the buckles on their patent-leather shoes. When I look back steadily only one woman is there, and she is a stranger.

She is, perhaps, twenty-six or seven, tall, dark, heavy, none too clean; what my mother, with her English eye for distinctions, calls 'common'. She has just fallen down in the street and been brought in until she feels well enough to go on. She is flopped in one of our squatter's chairs with her dirty stockinged feet up on the arms, and my mother is giving her a cup of tea – in a cup and saucer from our breakfast set – while Cassie goes down to my grandmother's for Auntie Olga.

The woman is pregnant but I don't see that. What impresses

me about the woman is not her interesting condition but the interesting condition of her being there at all – the unlikeliness of her having got into the house by anything but extraordinary means. She has lit up an Ardath and is smoking. Nobody smokes in our house; certainly no lady has ever done so. Once settled with her feet up she seems so much at home that I wonder if she will ever move. (And in fact in my memory she never does. She goes on sitting there for ever.) It is her looking so settled in a place where she should never have been that strikes me, and makes her, in retrospect, the only possessor, the permanent occupant, of that particular chair. She is the only person I can actually see there.

I suppose she must have left eventually. I do not recall it. What I recall is that when my Auntie Olga of the V.A.D.s arrived, and found her smoking, she was delivered a fearful lecture on the dangers of nicotine to unborn infants and told to stub the thing out immediately.

She does, fiercely, on the arm of the chair, and at the same time she utters a word I have never heard outside the schoolyard or in the remotest corners of under-the-house. It is a word that twenty years later will be commonplace; but back there it punches such a hole in the clear fabric of things that I might have looked right through it into the future and seen a whole new generation, a different world.

She has stumbled into the wrong decade, this young woman – that too constitutes her 'interesting condition'. She is a ghost of the future. No wonder my mother looks appalled.

But there she is, tall, dark, heavy, none too clean and pregnant; making the canvas sag with her weight. And there she remains, an obstacle I have to step around for ever after, occupying our Front Verandah as solidly, as inevitably, as the chair she has made her own.

The Front Verandah ends at an invisible barrier which we children are forbidden to pass. Beyond, at the point where you can see along the side verandah into her room, it becomes Cassie's Verandah.

I am powerfully attracted. If there is something in Cassie's room, I reason, that my parents want to keep from me, it can only have to do with her ambiguous position among us. Cassie is close but she is not family. She comes from outside and has a family of her own, two sisters, both married, and a father from Harrisville who comes to visit her twice each year, a tall fellow, very spare and straight, with a moustache like the man on the Sloane's Liniment bottle. I have had occasion to observe and note his strangeness.

He has a little silver-handled pocket-knife, and I sat and watched him once, settled in his shirtsleeves on our back porch, with his boot-heels on the verandah rails and his chair tilted back in a manner that I knew would damage the legs, peel an apple and slice it into quarters, then into even thinner pieces which one by one he shook salt on and slowly chewed. When he saw me observing him, he paused, considered for a moment, then held out a slice.

I had never seen anyone eat an apple with salt before. It was a custom utterly foreign to me – outlandish. So that is what it means, I thought, to be *not family*.

Cassie works for us. When people ask me 'Is Cassie your

maid?' I vigorously deny it. We never refer to her as that. My grandmother calls Della, the big dim-witted, one-toothed girl who slaves in her kitchen behind the shop, 'the maid'. It isn't nice. Cassie cooks and cleans for us and is paid twenty-two and six a week, plus board. She is my mother's help and confidante and her ally against the aunts. She eats her meals with us and loves us as her own, but is anomalous. She has her own room, her own life, which we are forbidden to enter or even to look into from a distance, and a gentleman friend, Cassie's Jack, a forty-five year-old veteran of Gallipoli and the Somme who is Dublin-born and does odd jobs for the nuns up at Mt Mary's. (One day in the near future they will marry. Cassie will leave us, and then, after yet another of my father's renovations, come back to live on her verandah in a little two-roomed, self-contained flat.)

Cassie's Room belongs to the life she lives apart from us, across clear boundaries that begin and end at seven o'clock at night and seven the following morning, and other, less clear but equally inviolable, that begin at some point, far to the left along the Front Verandah, where you might get a look into her room. I test the point continually. Can I *see*? *Now* can I? It is easy to let a little car, once its wheels have been wound up, go whizzing, all of its own accord, too far along the floorboards, and find the barrier is merely notional and can be crossed.

I cross it. Determined to get to the source of at least one mystery, I go further. In a moment of extravagant bravado I break into Cassie's Room – I am maybe four years old and it is not difficult, the door is wide open – and am deeply dis-appointed. It smells different, that is true, but I cannot isolate the source of the smell. If there is something forbidden here I can't lay my hands on it. There is no mystery. After poking about for a bit I find a jar of Pond's cold cream. I remove the lid, sniff, use a finger: a honey smell. And since Cassie is associated in my mind with things to eat, I sit cross-legged on the floor, and in a ritual the simplest savage would understand, set myself solemnly, steadily, to swallow the stuff to the last sickly dollop.

My sister and I have no room of our own in this earlier house. We sleep in home-made cots on the verandah beyond our parents' bedroom window, where we are in easy reach.

The verandah is closed on that side by a fernery, or, as I see it, opens on that side into it. Diagonal slats of unpainted timber gone grey with age are hung with stag horns, elk horns, orchids that sprout from fleshy knobs, and shaggy wire baskets of hare's foot and maidenhair. The ground is all sword-ferns round a pond with three opulent goldfish. Behind it is a kind of grotto made of pinkish-grey concrete, a dozen scaly branches of which, eaten raw in places, droop and tangle like the arms, half-petrified, half-rotting, of a stranded sea monster.

The Fernery scares me. Being taken out of the house each night and set to sleep beside it is like being put down at the edge of a rain-forest. Those stag horns, huge blunt-nosed decapitations, those hairy fern-stalks with flesh-pale coils at the end, go too far back to the primordial damp and breath of things. If I step out there, I think, in my sleep for instance, sleep-walking, I will get time-lost, I will turn back into some smooth or hairy green thing with dirt in my fists.

I fiercely resent our sleeping arrangements. I have the strong sense, when we are put to bed out there, however much hugging and kissing we are allowed, and last trips to the bathroom, and last drinks of water, that we are being abandoned, shut out, not only from the continuing life of the house, which goes on well past the boundary of our seven o'clock bedtime (for my parents play bridge in the evening, and over a late supper of savoury biscuits and cake exchange what I take to be the real news of the day), but from the house itself, that secure enclosure.

A verandah is not part of the house. Even a child knows this. It is what allows travelling salesmen, with one foot on the step to heave their cases over the threshold and show their wares with no embarrassment on either side, no sense of privacy violated. It has allowed my mother, with her strict notion of the forms, to bring a perfect stranger in off the street and settle her (for ever as it happens) in one of our squatter's chairs. Verandahs are no-man's-land, border zones that keep contact with the house and its activities on one face but are open on the other to the street, the night and all the vast, unknown areas beyond.

I reject my cot and refuse to stay there. I become a night wanderer, a rebel nomad trailing my blanket through the house to my favourite camping places: behind the Hall Door (where I can squinny through a crack and watch the card-play, and overhear – what? what?); between wireless and wall in the Piano Room. Though when I wake in the morning I am always outside again, at the edge of the Fernery, behind the bars of my cot.

Perhaps it is this daily experience of being cast out and then let in again that has made the house and all its rooms so precious to me. Each morning I step across the threshold and there it is, a world recovered, restored.

[III]

The main door of the house, beyond the Front Verandah, is of stained cedar, with brass locks and door knob and lights of a milky-blue jellyfish colour. It is kept permanently open with a stopper, an outsized frog.

To the right, down a hallway with a Persian runner, is the bedroom where my parents sleep. Their door too is always open, it being a convention in these houses that nothing is seen or heard that is not meant to be. The convention soon becomes a habit. Air circulates from room to room through a maze of interconnecting spaces; every breath can be heard, every creak of a bed-post or spring; you sleep, in the humid summer nights, outside the sheet and with as little clothing as decency allows; and yet privacy is perfectly preserved. A training in perception has as much to do with what is ignored and passed over as with what is observed. You see what you are meant to see. You hear when you are called.

Beyond our parents' room is the spare room where visitors are put, and where in the early afternoon, like most ladies, our mother takes her nap, sometimes with my sister and me beside her.

On the other side of the Hall, opening immediately off it through an archway with pierced slats in the spandrels and occupying the whole of that half of the house, is our Front Room, a big high-ceilinged room with hexagonal silk lamp-shades fringed with gold, sash windows at knee height that are heavily curtained and stuck with paint, and stained panelling to the plate rack, beyond which, like the rest of the interior, it is tongue-and-groove.

On the wall opposite my parents' bed is a framed picture of the Sacred Heart of Jesus, a real oil painting so thickly varnished that its medium seems like the coagulated darkness of another world, which the Jesus figure, with hollow cheeks and a pained but forgiving expression, pushes through into the faint light of this one. The wall at that point, in a miraculous way that defies mere geography, is open to another order of reality and an atmosphere so heavy that it might be difficult to breathe. Just looking into the frame makes you breathless. Any illumination in there comes from the Sacred Heart itself, a metal object, perfectly symmetrical, radiant with some sort of extraterrestrial magnetism and proclaiming its brand name in incandescent gold.

The picture dominates the room. Not because of its luminosity, which is intense, or the power of its subject (however bizarre it may be to have a metal heart glowing out of your rib cage, and to be pointing to it with a burning finger), or because of Our Lord's grave expression ('a yard and a half of misery', my mother would call it – it is just the sort of face my sister and I could never get away with), but because the painting, like Jesus himself, is an intrusion.

A wedding present from my father's family, it is the source of deep resentment. My mother is a non-Catholic. It was only with the greatest reluctance that she signed us over, before we were born, to the Church. The Sorrowful Witness has been spirited into our parents' bedroom by my grandmother, as a kind of celestial superintendent or voyeur. He gazes perpetually down over the foot of the bed out of His other world; not disapproving but head-on-side-regretful, and with the light streaming out of that heart-shaped appliance like a torchbeam that will never be turned off.

Though it has no door, and the knee-high window to our verandah is always raised, we have learned early, my sister and I, that this room is not to be trespassed upon. Its thresholds are magic barriers.

The drawers of our mother's dressing-table are full of temptations to small hands, and all its crystal is breakable. She keeps her private treasures here in a marvellous tangle of chains, ribbons, hairpieces, silver-mesh evening bags, and in several boxes, none of them locked. One is of ivory. It contains her family heirlooms, a seal of my grandfather's and Grandma's Victorian jewellery. Another has compartments for a little set of scales and a jar of dried-up *aqua fortis*. These come from the days when our mother, as a carefree girl of nineteen or twenty, went gold-buying with a married sister, all through the country towns of Southern Queensland in an open Hup. Yet another, a cigar box, is stacked with the Christmas and birthday cards (too many) of our father's courtship.

On one side of the dressing-table is my mother's cut-crystal dressing-table set – stoppered scent bottle and atomiser, two heavy bowls, one diamond-shaped for jewellery, the round one for dusky powder and puff – and on the other the spirit lamp she keeps burning in memory of her departed parents. It shows a real light, a milky glow, unliked the garish painted one of the

Sacred Heart, and she tends it, pouring in the methylated spirits, trimming the wick, with a piety that might, if I understood, tell me a good deal about what she most deeply believes. (When we left Edmondstone Street she gave up the little lamp – we didn't take the Sacred Heart to the new house either – and my mother, I thought, was changed. She seemed freed at last of a whole troop of ghosts, including the ghost of England, that in our first house had kept her constrained. But by then, of course, the whole world had changed. The war was over, the old pieties were dying; we had entered a new and freer age.)

It strikes me now that that house was not simply the house of my own childhood, as I have so far presented it, but a house of children. Even my parents are more like older children playing Mothers and Fathers than real adults: she the dutiful daughter and keeper of the flame, he his mother's boy, still referring to my grandmother's house as 'down home', and still in thrall, for all his male assurance, to that small, soft, demanding woman who two or three times a week sends up his favourite dishes, the old-country cabbage-rolls and sweet things my mother does not cook. He lives with us but Grandma's is his address. She still insists that the postman leave his letters there, and he collects them on his way from work.

A decade later my mother will become a power in her own right, a business woman of extraordinary daring and flair; but in the days of the Sacred Heart and the little spirit lamp she is in the shadows, and I see now that she must often have raged inwardly with a sense of herself as powerfully unused, with energies she could not express in the polite round of social duties she was limited to, shopping expeditions to the Sales, morning tea at department stores with the Girls. Perhaps it is for this reason that she seems, in retrospect, childishly wilful at times, and spoiled, and why my father, though essentially a strong man, is so soft with her. I see them, in their big bed with the rounded shell-like ends, and under the gaze of the Sorrowful Watcher, as child conspirators, snatching what freedom they can from the grown-ups. Though there were occasions as well when my father's loyalties went the other way and he sided (we could feel it in the aggrieved silences with which my mother filled the house; she was a great sulker) with my grandmother and the league of aunts.

So my mother's room was both hers and not hers. Nor was it my father's. They might, in their different ways, have felt the same trepidation on entering it, the same sense of bold trespass, that we children did. It was already too fully occupied.

All the more astonishing then, the innocence, or plain effrontery, of Our Burglar, a young fellow of unknown age and appearance who, one morning early in the war, picked the lock on the Side Door, found his way in the dark to my parents' bedroom, and – impudently undismayed by the presence of the Sorrowful Watcher and impervious, it seems, to the magic of thresholds – entered, crept quietly over the creaky floorboards to my father's lowboy, opened it, felt in along the second shelf among folded work shirts and pyjamas, and located our cash-box; an iron one about the size of a large sewing basket, but heavy, enamelled black, and with a combination lock.

He took it with him; but only as far as the Piano Room.

There, in the growing light, he discovered what I might have told him immediately, that the lock was broken – no need to screw your brow up and puzzle over numbers – and could be sprung with a thumb. He spilled the contents in a heap on the lino, and amateur that he was, must have been baffled, even enraged, to find nothing there but a few family documents. No cash. No jewels even. Just a fob watch of my father's which wasn't gold and two florin pieces that were no longer in circulation. He pocketed them and fled, leaving the cashbox open on the Piano Room floor, where Cassie would discover it on her early rounds; and was discovered himself, just after nine, at a George Street pawnshop. My father, whose name was on the watch, was called to the police station to see him, but declined to lay a charge.

'What was he like?' I demanded.

'Oh, an ordinary young feller,' my father told us. 'I felt sorry for him.'

Ordinary! I was appalled.

Burglars obsessed me at that time. I had known for ever that one of them would come one day, and used to get up when all the rest of the household was asleep to check the windows and try the doors. Darkness to me was the abode of burglars. They were abroad in every street. I had already created in imagination the one who would choose some day to fulfil the deepest of my fearful expectations. I expected him to be bold at least – maybe monstrous. But that he should appear at last and arouse nothing in my father but pity! I was affronted. I set myself to observe the fellow, not through my father's eyes but with my own. I imagined myself waking in the early hours, peering round the frame of the verandah window and catching him there in the otherworldly glow of the Sacred Heart. He was wearing sandshoes (it was the only detail my father could supply) and was feeling his way among flannel pyjamas towards the cold metal of the cashbox, while Jesus – sorrowful – pointed helpfully to his own metal heart, as if to say, 'Go deeper. It *is* there – a bit to the left.' 'Ah,' says the burglar to himself as his hand finds an edge, 'so it is.'

I follow him then to the Piano Room. He is sitting cross-legged on the floor, sorting quickly through the tumbled contents, and when he glances up and finds me in the door frame gravely watching, he motions me to be quiet but is not otherwise disturbed. (And why should he be? If Sorrowful Jesus didn't put him off, why should a small boy in pyjama bottoms, standing on one foot at the door – or does he believe I am his accomplice? Am I? When I checked the key to the Side Door, did I, unconsciously, turn it to the left instead of the right?)

I step in over the threshold and squat beside him. I am full of questions.

What are you looking for? It's only papers, you know – our school reports, birth certificates, and the watch doesn't go. How do you dare to do it – just walk into other people's houses like that, in the dark, while they're asleep? Aren't you scared? Aren't you?

Piss off, he tells me, but without much force. He's such a mild young fellow. I despise him.

So once at least, just to see how it might be done, I go to the Side Door myself, and following what I think might be his route, creep barefooted down the hallway, cross the threshold of my parents' room – on tiptoe, daring the magic, one big toe at a time – and am just at the foot of their bed, in the full glare of the Sacred Heart, when my father starts awake.

'For heaven's sake,' he shouts, 'what are you up to now?' Then more quietly, as an afterthought: 'Is he sleep-walking?'

I put my hands out in front of me, close my eyes, and pretend, but it's no go.

'Stop that,' my mother tells me, snapping the light on. 'What's the matter? Do you want the lav?'

So if my parents' room remains a place of mysteries, it is because of its intruders, though it is the second, Our Burglar, who impresses me more: that young fellow in sandshoes, his features a blank, who has so quickly solved the maze of our house and gone straight to its centre. It disturbs me that the face of Jesus should be so familiar (I could pick Him out in any line-up) while Our Burglar's remains forever secret and dim. My father has seen him and found him ordinary. Which means only, perhaps, that he has no eye for things, or no powers of description. What does ordinary mean?

[IV]

At the end of the Hall, across a wide crossways passage, lies what we call the Piano Room after the big iron-framed instrument that is its major presence. A solid upright of German make, with bronze candleholders and a fretwork swing for the music, it is topped by two splendid jardinières. They are identical but only the one on the left has a name. This is the Brass Jardinière, and it is the focus of such passionate attention on my part that I think of it as shining brighter than the other (as if my thoughts had power just in themselves to burnish by contact), though it is Cassie's duty to see that they get equal attention from her elbow each Monday morning, and equal amounts of Brasso on a chamois cloth.

The Piano Room is my favourite room in the house. It is where we are most often to be found – we children, my mother, Cassie and the occasional visitor – in the long afternoons, since it is shaded by the leaves of an enormous mango and is always cool. It is where we gather each evening to listen to the wireless and hear the news, and where, quietly playing while my mother and Cassie exchange bits and pieces of talk, almost not listening and too young as yet to be sent out of the room, I pick up other news as well, the secrets and half-secrets of the world of women. Soon after this it will be closed to me for ever; and even now sometimes, with a glance in my direction, my mother or Maisie or one of the others will slip into code. But little minds are quick. I am skilled at the art of overhearing. Besides, I have learned in this room to listen to music. You let it fill your mind; but what you follow, under variations, is the tune.

My mother plays a little; poorly, but enough to provide an accompaniment when there is a sing-song on Sunday nights. That is, when five or six friends, in those innocent days before the war, link arms and harmonise from an illuminated sheet. The picture I have of them is clear in outline but fuzzy with sentiment – not all of it mine. That is why I have used the word 'innocent' of days that were neither more nor less so than any other. I mean it to express feeling rather than fact. For what they are recreating, these people, or so I now see, is some earlier moment when they were all younger. The quality of nostalgia in the image is in them rather than in my memory of them; they exist in several dimensions of time. These youngish people, now dead, are my parents; they belong, even as they evoke their youth, to another generation, and they seem old to me (though in fact they are younger than I am now) because they *are* my parents, and because the clothes they are wearing, Fair Isle sweaters and pleated slacks, georgette blouses, strapped shoes, are ones that will be out of date when I grow up. The songs they are singing are out of date already: 'Love's Old Sweet Song'.

(Our father also plays, but only in octaves and by ear. He plays for us children: soldiers' songs from the Great War.)

I have my first lessons on this piano, practising for half an hour twice a day. But the instrument is too grand and imposing, has locked up in it too much power, for my stiff-fingered stumblings or my parents' bland simplicities. Only when my mother's sister, Aunt Frances comes, does it reveal itself. The result is almost frightening.

Aunt Frances is a 'real pianist'. Twenty years older than my mother, she learned to play as one of the accomplishments of a middle-class young lady in the nineteenth century. It is a century to which she still belongs.

As a girl, it seems, she was a beauty. My grandfather, a well-to-do fruit merchant, was excessively proud of her. He took her to first nights of all the shows and light operas, *The Quaker Girl, Les Cloches de Cornville*, bought her the sheet music next day, and treated her generally 'like a princess in a fairy tale'. (This is a phrase I hear over and over when my mother retells the story. She is evoking a time she never knew.) But the princess fell from grace. She ran off with a cousin, breaking several laws, and became in consequence the first of my mother's people to come to Australia; in the beginning to Lightning Ridge, then to a tent at Mount Morgan. Things went badly in both places, and when her husband, who was too spoiled to find regular work, took to mending clocks and watches, she had to supplement their income by giving lessons in piano, fiddle and mandoline. All this, of course, was years back. When I first knew her she was already sixty, a tiny person with a beehive of silver hair, not at all the sort of woman, you might have thought, to break even one law – till you heard her play. Very gentle but easily offended, she had notions of austere gentility that awed my father, though he was very fond of her, and must have made my mother feel at times that she had failed her parents and all of us by not keeping up. (She did keep up, of course, but was it by English standards enough?)

My mother was the baby of her family by many years.

When she came to Australia she was thirteen, just the age perhaps when it is most difficult to make a change. She clung to what she had left or lost and was more English than any of her brothers, who had all been grown men when they migrated and who prided themselves now on being local boys. English for my mother was right. She reproduced in our childhood what she remembered (minus a few housemaids) of her own life in Edwardian London. We ate the same food, heard the same little tags and sayings ('Hark at the boy!' my mother would say; or scornfully, of one of my father's no-hoper friends: 'He's not got tuppence to jingle on a tombstone') and were given the same old-fashioned remedies against winter ills. Forbidden to use local slang, or to speak or act 'Australian', we grew up as in a foreign land, where everything local, everything outside the house that was closest and most ordinary, had about it the glow of the exotic. The effect on me was just the opposite of what my mother must have hoped. 'Gimme,' I would snarl when my sister and I were out of earshot – playing Australian and tough; or 'I'm goin' t' th' dunny'; or, with shocking self-consciousness, 'Him and me done it this arvo. I betcha we did.' My ideal was one of those freckled, red-headed kids who burned at the beach and got blisters and had to wear a shirt into the water. (I liked the look of the shirt when it stuck in some places, showing the pink skin, and bubbled blue in others.) I even longed for the real Australian rubbish in other families' yards: beer cartons, the straw jackets that Fourex bottles came in, the stack of 'dead marines' waiting for the bottle-oh on the back porch. The smell of stale beer, which my mother abominated, was especially authentic.

(Once, when my father is organising a float for one of the war parades, we have three soldiers in the house who are to appear on the back of one of his lorries with sandbags and unloaded tommy-guns. The youngest is a freckled fellow with wavy red-gold hair, and in the afternoon, when they are lounging about waiting to be called, half-asleep with the heat and the beer they have been given, I climb on to his knee and push my face up to his. The boy must think I am trying to kiss him. Drowsily, to humour me, he responds. But I know nothing of kissing. I am intoxicating myself with his strangeness, the smell of Fourex on his breath.)

'So what is it to be?' says Aunt Frances. 'The Battle of the Nations?' As if she had to ask! It is my favourite. Also her own.

The illustrated sheet is coloured. It shows the charge of Napoleon's Old Guard, above it the grouped flags of the Allies. And the music itself, full of rumbly cannon fire in the bass, the clash and tangle of cavalry charges, snatches of anthems, has so entered my imagination by the time I am six or seven years old that I can follow the progress of that momentous affair, reduced as it is to purely musical terms, in all its shifts and changing fortunes and flashes of light through smoky cloud. It never fails to fire me to a pitch of breathless excitement.

'Here comes the Old Guard,' Aunt Frances shouts, leaning low over the keyboard as she plunges into 'La Marseillaise'.

'And here comes Wellington!' I yell at the turn into the climax.

I can read these entries in the music, the legs of the massed horses in waves of semiquavers, almost before I can read a book, and am allowed sometimes to take the music out and follow the battle in my head. I know every note. And even if I didn't, the sheets themselves would excite me. The title has such a powerful effect on my imagination that it creates a music of its own.

How grand it sounds: 'The Battle of the Nations'. So final. So universal. Like 'The Great War'. It gives me a shivery feeling and a special view of history – a series of dramatic climaxes and resolutions, all shot through with coloured uniforms, patriotic tunes, torn flags; a view that is inherent as well in certain words from the books I like to read, 'Age' and 'Era', and in such phrases as 'the day hung in the balance' or 'the field was won'. So that I feel a subtle shift of meaning when the real war, our war, begins and 'the Great War' becomes simply 'The Last War'; as if history, that closed book, had suddenly been opened again, or we had been turned right about so that what lay before us wasn't the clear past but an entirely unpredictable future.

I did not mistake the horrors of what was happening in Europe – I had seen too many newsreels for that. But I did not reject 'The Battle of the Nations' either. What I saw now was that it belonged to another form than documentary, that its events, as I knew them, had taken place not at Leipzig but at the same place on another planet – which is to say, in a language that can be heard and read, and which the body responds to as immediately as to taste or touch, but which no one has ever spoken on this one. It is a language of the spirit, that comes out of people's fingertips more than their mouths and is locked up as well in furniture. From which it can be beaten or stroked or strummed.

What astonishes me now is not the pictures I see when Aunt Frances strikes up 'The Battle of the Nations' – the heroic visions – but the mystery that is involved in my experiencing anything at all: my actually hearing and making sense of this disembodied language that has to break out of a physical body before it can be expressed, but is contained as well – the cannon fire and carnage of 'The Battle of the Nations', but also *Traümerei, Liebestraum* and an infinity of other events and states of being – in our suburban upright. The piano is a magic box. But we too are magic boxes. That is the revelation.

Compared with this, that modern miracle the Wireless seems a poor thing, entirely earthbound. I have begun to be interested in the inner working of things and 'wireless' puzzles me, since it is the fact of its actually *having* wires, all wonderfully stretched and pegged to a frame, that makes the Piano capable of flight. The Wireless is limited to what is actual and mundane: the unpredictable happenings of the nightly News.

Still, as a piece of furniture it is impressive, you can't deny it: three feet high with three kinds of veneer and a speaker whose shape you can feel behind knobbly cloth. The voices that come from it owe as much of their significance, surely, to the rich solidity of the thing, its oneness with tables and beds and chairs, as to their own rounded vowels or the importance (for the course of World History depends on it) of what they have to report. Much of what we come to feel about the war, and our own present and precarious fate, might be different if the instrument itself were different. If it were made of some metal alloy, for example, rather than living wood. Or if it were small enough, as now, to be one of the body's light appendages. A degree of gravity, at this moment, is essential. The Wireless has it. We are in the age of certainties. Its three veneers, the baroque curves it shares with wardrobes and sideboards, its bourgeois dignity, are terms we appreciate. It gives a visible presence, a tangible form, to words that might otherwise, in this quiet backwater, have nothing to attach themselves to.

Freedom. Destiny. The easy life we have grown up in, white for the most part, British almost entirely, in spirit Protestant, has never been under threat. If there are those among us whose freedom has been lost, who have been dispossessed, we do not see them. They are invisible – like the aborigines, who have not yet established themselves in our consciousness. Or they have not yet arrived, even if they are already living down the road or next door – like the migrants, whose sorrows we do not hear because we have not yet opened our ears to receive them.

The Wireless commands attention because it is 'furniture'. We draw our chairs up and attend. And this sitting together in a family group, drawn here by the furniture itself, is part of the message we are to receive.

We do not know it yet but the war is already won.

The other thing we do not know is that all the values it was meant to embody, even in us, are already lost.

On top of the piano, left and right, the jardinières, existing less in their own metal form, for all the bronze glow they give off from constant polishing, than in the volume they displace in my head; which is different in each case, since what they contain is different.

The one on the right contains needles, buttons, button-cards, reels of cotton in various colours, more cards with rows of press-studs and hooks and eyes, and a couple of bobbins. It is my mother's slapdash version of a sewing-basket.

On two or three afternoons a week, when she can't put it off, she and Cassie sit here darning socks, mending rips in our play clothes and sewing buttons on the flies of my father's work trousers.

My mother is a hopeless seamstress. I see her struggling with the thick flannel, making a botch as usual; tearing threads with her teeth, using her thumb to push down an untidy mound of muddled stitches, sighing, tossing the thing on to the finished pile to take up a sock. Cassie meanwhile will be reading aloud. They take it in turns to read, chapter by chapter, from my mother's favourite books, the ones she read in her youth, and I come to know several novels in this fashion: *David Copperfield*, which has provided me with my name (it isn't family – it comes from literature), *John Halifax, Gentleman*, *The Channings*, *The Manxman*, *Jane Eyre*.

Not every afternoon was spent like this. The weather was mostly good and we were active outdoors children for the most part, eager to play on so long as we could see a ball against the rapidly falling dark, and only reluctantly answering the call to come in and get washed for tea. There were days after school when we mucked about under the house, exploring, testing ourselves against the darkness down there, pushing ourselves to the limits of our young courage in outrageous dares; other days when we picked teams and played rounders in the yard, or Donkey, branding one another with a bald tennis ball, or if girls were in the majority, Statues, in which we froze, when time stopped, in unbalanced attitudes. But when I think back to that time it is in the Piano Room that I find myself most fully present and absorbed; letting the words fall into my ear that most clearly 'tell me things'.

Time back there has a different consistency; we move through it at a different pace. And nothing brings it back to my senses with such rich immediacy as those long afternoons when a needle drawn back and forth through heavy flannel is the real measure of it, a steady crossing and recrossing, or words out of those voluminous novels as they fall into the room in the differing voices of those two women: my mother's English voice with its slight London accent, Cassie's Australian one of the farmgirl from Harrisville, crossing and recrossing to give their own texture to things. If time seems different it is because we measure it, back there, by other coefficients, have different images for it, experience it in bodies whose blood is richer (which is why we are susceptible to boils), and sluggish with other and heavier food. (Or is this a child's view of time, like the child's view of space, in which everything appears larger than it was?) Either way, I think of those afternoons, between the end of school and six o'clock teatime, as endless, their hours so densely packed with experience and events that time appears viscous. It rolls rather than flows, meeting a perceptible resistance, as those Victorian sentences, in their difficult unfolding, seem always to hold back from conclusion, suspending you, impatient for the end but breathlessly subdued, in the stream of your own attention, so that you grow light-headed and wide-eyed drowsy, as if the mere effort of listening had laid a spell on your limbs. You wake after an hour to find you have passed whole years of someone else's life – in England, in another century, and now, abruptly, it is half-past five by the hall clock in this one. Quickly the book is closed and put on top of the Piano, with a thread to mark our place. Our father is expected. The sound of his truck is like the arrival of Zeus in a thunderclap. The whole day immediately changes, its light, the pace of things. Needles, cards, cotton-reels – all the paraphernalia of female occupations – are bundled anyhow into the right-hand jardinière, and my mother, released, flies out to meet him. She is utterly transformed.

The other jardinière, the one on the left, is perhaps my favourite object in the house. A deep mystery hovers about it, and if anyone were to remind me that it is in fact indistinguishable from the other I would deny it.

The right-hand jardinière is utterly mundane. Anyone can see that. The left-hand one is transfigured by its contents. I would know it blindfold. I would be drawn to it infallibly by the heat of my own passionate fingerprints.

It is the place in our house where a thing is put (and searched for) when there is nowhere else for it to go, a general repository of the half-lost, the half-found, the useless-for-the-time-being-but-not-quite-rejected, and all those bits and pieces, and odd things and marvels that have no formal category.

'Put it in the Brass Jardinière,' my mother tells me when I come to her with some small object she has no use for, something indefinable, impossible, but which she doesn't want to disappoint me by refusing.

'Have a look in the Brass Jardinière,' she suggests when the impossible is just what I cannot do without.

On rainy afternoons when we have to stay in, or when they want, quite simply, to get rid of me, I am sent off to look in the jardinière for something no one expects me to find there, though I never complain or give up hope.

The Brass Jardinière is the measure of my belief in the world's infinite plenitude, its capacity to reproduce itself in a multitude of forms. It never fails me. It is such a pleasure, such a blossoming of the spirit, just to climb onto the piano seat, reach up and get your arms around the thing, lift it carefully down, and then, in pretty much the same spot where Our Burglar emptied the contents of the cashbox, upend it on the lino; or, better still, to reach in and empty it in promiscuous handfuls 'and to see what is there'.

Everything is there: everything odd. One baby's bootee a little rusty with age, the top off a Schaeffer fountain-pen, one cup from a doll's tea-set without the saucer; the gold chain off an evening bag, one grey kid glove without a button, half a *diamanté* clasp, the slice of mother-of-pearl that is one side of a penknife handle; odd earrings and collar-studs – all things that have been put there over the years in the hope that the other half will turn up and make a pair. The spirit of accidental separation hovers over the jardinière, but in so far as it is itself part of a pair, it speaks for completeness, for final restitution.

I lay all the objects out in their kinds, then check for the hundredth time that no mistake has been made. It is a game that is never finished, since who knows, next time some change may have occurred – not in the objects themselves but in the relationship between them. Deeply serious, it is a game that demands all my concentration. I am playing God.

I try to memorise what the jardinière contains, to keep all this rubbish in my head, so that if, in poking about the house, or under it, or out in the backyard, I should come across 'the other one', I can restore both objects to use. I refuse to accept that this mortuary of lost couples is really the end. I dedicate myself. I imagine going through life with the jardinière invisibly in my arms, a heavy burden; which is why I have begun the long business of committing its contents to memory. This is a secret. But the real secret is the source of my commitment. As a smaller child than I am now I had an invisible friend, a lost twin of my own. I cling to the jardinière in the belief that one day we too may be united: that he (or is it I?) will be found.

[v]

It is a forest under here. Regularly spaced, the stumps have grey, galvanised-iron caps and are painted with creosote to keep off white ants.

Seen from the washtubs, it slopes steeply upwards towards the Front Verandah; but you can also see it another way: as existing in a perspective in which the distance from first stump to last isn't at all commensurate with the house above but is to be judged by the tallness of the stumps behind you and their littleness far off. It might be miles. It is a forest that stretches for miles, as dark as anything in Grimm and belonging to the geography of the body's hot experience of it rather than to Australia or South Brisbane. It is its own place.

Reason tells me that it can only be the same length as our hall. But reason has nothing to do with it. The coefficients of measurement are in each case different, as a room filled with sunlight has different measurements from the same room in the dark.

The forest under the house is measured by the time it takes, on hands and knees, to crawl from your father's toolshed to the place, far up under the Front Verandah, where the floorboards are so close to the earth that you can barely squeeze in. By that and the expanding darkness in your lungs that is partly breathlessness, partly fear, and partly the terrible downward pressure of the house itself, all its rooms of furniture, on the air above you, and what it takes to keep it hanging there by an act of will.

The whole space is closed in with vertical slats, painted nigger-brown on the outside and black within. Old bed frames with rusty springs are stacked against one wall, and later the cast-iron from our Front Verandah. Cinders have been spread over the topsoil, but if you scratch a little you find earth. It is black, rather. And if you scratch further you come upon debris, bits of broken china, bent forks, old tin pannikins, encrusted nails and pins, which suggest that habitation here might go back centuries. History tells us, of course, that it does not (we discount the abos), but I don't believe it. History belongs to the world of light. The debris under the cinders, under the thin topsoil of under-the-house, bears the same relation to history as the dark of our stump forest to the lighted rooms above. They belong to different dimensions.

Against the slats of the back wall stand washing tubs, with a washboard bleached white with suds and a mangle. To the left, in an open space by the kitchen stairs, is a round stone fireplace, much blackened, with a copper, and on the wall beside it a long dribble of powdery blue where the blue-bag is hung. Here, every Monday morning, Mrs Allen hefts steaming sheets from boiler to washtubs on a three-foot stick.

Opposite, back under the house, is our father's toolshed. It has a lattice door with a padlock, a concrete floor, and all round it at waist-level against the slab walls are benches. Screwed to one of them is a vice where in our own version of Chinese torture we experiment with fingerjoints and thumbs. Saws hang from nails. There are secateurs, clippers, wire-cutters, a reaping hook and, laid diagonally across one whole wall, a scythe. Chisels and screwdrivers, all graded by size, are in open trays, and smaller trays contain nails, hinges, wall-hooks, curtain rings. Our father is a neat workman and the whole place can be read at a glance.

There is also a book, the biggest I have ever seen. Nearly twelve inches thick and impossible to lift, it might, we think, be a guide to torture instruments, but is known as the Chinese Dictionary.

My sister and I are devoted to it. We spend long hours while my father files away at metal, or saws planks with one foot up on the trestle, seeking clues to how it might be deciphered or made use of. Earlier on we had great hopes of it; but they have faded as we discover that learning to read, in this case, has been no help at all. It refuses to open itself to us, and in so far as it has no boards, no title page, and the earliest pages are missing, we cannot even be sure that it *is* a dictionary, or even that it is Chinese, and our father cannot enlighten us. He is minding the book for a friend, who went off ages ago and has not come back.

From his toolroom, with the aid of a retired ship's carpenter called Pop or Old Jack, my father built the caravan we go away in at weekends, and since there is always one thing or another to be renovated or rebuilt, Old Jack is as permanent a figure under the house as Cassie is above. He is a smooth-skinned, nut-brown little fellow of seventy, perfectly bald and with a drooping nose, at the end of which there is always a rounding, opaque drop. He has perfected the art of planing a length of timber so that his clean sweep with the plane includes a sweep, as well, of his rolled sleeve across his nose, at the precise moment when the drop has gathered to a fullness and is about to fall.

Old Jack is an ancient mariner who knows no compulsion to confess. Closed, uncommunicative, but full of cryptic mutterings, he refuses to answer my questions about the ships he has been on – clipper-ships they might be, back in another century – or where he comes from or where he lives. If he has stories locked up in him he keeps them to himself. He barely speaks, even to my father. His only words are swear words, which down here have none of the shocking quality they might have upstairs. He directs them, as if this were the one language they could be expected to understand, to strayed hammers, snapped blades, nails that bend or go in crooked and planks with knots in them. Perhaps, I think, he has never discovered a tongue for addressing children, as we have never discovered a reading key for the Chinese dictionary. We are as cut off from him as if we belonged to another species. Baby whales.

Down here is the underside of things: the great wedge of air on which the house floats, ever darkness; the stumps of a forest of which the house, with its many rooms, forms the branches; a place whose dimensions are measured, not in ordinary feet and inches, but in heartbeats, or the number of seconds you can endure the sticky-soft lash of cobwebs against your mouth, or the weight of your body, at kneecap and palm, on crunchy cinders. It does not fit. The way a shadow may be bigger or smaller than the object that is casting it. There is room for error here, for movement, for escape. So you crawl down here when the ordinary feet and inches of the house, its fixed times and rules, will not fit. Or when *you* won't. There are no clocks down here. There is not even language. They have not yet been invented. To come down here, up under the floorboards and the life of rooms, is to enter a dream space, dark, full of terrors that lurk behind tree-trunks in the thickest forest, hob-goblins, old gods, but full as well of the freedom and mystery of a time before houses – the old-new, gloomy-glad world where hammers and nails and planks of wood are inhabited by spirits that listen and respond, and where bodies, with no awareness of space or time, expand, contract, float, lapse into dreaming.

In bed at night, at the very edge of sleep, you feel that there may after all be a balance to things: that the underdark outside matches now, but perfectly, the dark within . . .

[VI]

But I see now that I have passed over something, the Front Room. I have allowed it, in the otherwise orderly progress of my description, to be displaced by the more attractive and interesting Piano Room; and that is appropriate perhaps, since that is how things also stood in our life. The Front Room is a dead room. Nothing happens there. We never enter it. And there is something odd in this, since of all the rooms in the house it is the most accessible, the most immediately visible.

It opens directly off the Hall, through an archway springing from square wooden pedestals on each of which, perfectly reflecting one another as in a mirror, stand double figures in burnished spelter, an elongated youth, barefoot and naked, but saved from immodesty by the fortuitous play of his companion's garments, and a female figure, equally graceful, who might be his twin. She runs beside him in a short tunic that clings to her breasts like wet silk and plays round her lower body like flame.

The youth's hair is shoulder-length and wild. He would pass, decades later, for an idealised surfie. The girl's is waist-length and falls in tresses loosely tangled. On narrow feet of an extraordinary refinement they are making their way out of a thicket of life-sized vineleaves, all veined and serrated, which as they wind upward with corkscrew tendrils produce electric lamps, two to a branch in russet gold.

These figures, classical in inspiration but playfully decadent in form, are not purely decorative – if they were they would be indecent – and their presence has nothing to do with the shedding of a merely physical light. They are admonitory, and I know them at a glance. With their parted lips and soft, lovesick eyes, they do not look harried, but they have their back to the Front Room and are fleeing. They can only be Adam and Eve under the angel's sword. Interpreted thus, they confirm my vision of the room as a place of forbidden delights, a pleasure garden that is denied even to my parents, since they too never venture there.

Carefully composed and grandly furnished, with a Genoa-velvet lounge suite, sideboards with barley-sugar legs and little glass-topped occasional tables, its three sash windows hung with curtains of a dusky-pink colour, with ropes and tassels of gold, our Front Room is a show place.

Beside each of the three Genoa-velvet lounge-chairs is a smoker's stand, polished brass with a cut-glass bowl. In one, the column is plain but the tray is embossed at the rim with lilies; the others, a pair, have plain trays but the columns are liquorice-twists. On the bow-fronted sideboard, which matches a dining-table and chairs, is an array of glassware, all Webb and Corbett crystal: a whisky set with straight-sided glasses and a square decanter, a sherry set with stemmed glasses and a decanter like a giant teardrop, and a silver cocktail-shaker with swizzle sticks whose tops represent the suits in a pack of cards. All these objects, the three smoker's stands, the drinking sets, the cocktail-shaker, are wedding presents; their display is obligatory. But they are also clues I decide, after long thought, to what our Front Room has been set up for and why we are forbidden to go there.

My parents do not smoke or drink, and my mother, though a passionate and daring bridge-player, who will go no trumps on nothing, is dead set against all forms of gambling.

Our Front Room is a warning, richly put, against easy pleasures and the dangers of 'the social life'. The instruments of smoking and drinking are made visible, displayed and kept in a state of awful glitter; but only to demonstrate their attractiveness, and to show how firmly, in this house, they are resisted.

I don't believe I ever saw my parents take into that room anyone they valued as a friend or genuinely respected. Business acquaintances who expected to be offered liquor might be sat there for a time, as in the lounge of a theatre. All the lights would be lit, including the red lamps of warning at the entrance, and we would come in our pyjamas and slippers to see whoever it was, uncomfortably ensconced in one of the armchairs and sipping an inch of Brown Muscat or Tawny Port. Only Cassie had the freedom of the place, and even she never faced it unless armed with a carton full of dusters. Once a week, all the carpets, chairs and curtains were beaten, the smokers' stands brought up with Brasso, and the crystal glasses polished with a cloth. Then the lights were put out and we turned our backs on it.

There could be (this too I saw clearly) no door to such a place – even a door like all the others in the house that was kept permanently open. The whole point was in its being visible at all times, so that we had, in going down the hall, to see its many temptations glowing subtly in the dark.

Beyond the Front Room was the door that led to the passage and the rooms at the back of the house; and at the end of this passage, on the left, was the Side Door through which, in his own good time, Our Burglar would get in.

It was another heavy door, whose glass had been covered with oiled paper in a geometrical pattern: squares superimposed to make eight-sided stars. Outside, a porch, from which stairs led down to the drive. The bottom step was where I was sent to collect the lettuces, tomatoes, egg-plants, radishes and beans that my grandfather left on his way home from his garden patch.

But I was connected to this door by something deeper than my ordinary comings and goings. I was, in those days, a prodigious bleeder. At the least provocation my nose became a bloody fountain, and Cassie's quick folk cure was to lay me flat on my back and slip the Side Door Key under my sweater, a heavy black key about five inches long that smelled of iron or dried blood.

It was meant, I suppose, to work by physical suggestion, or a kind of sympathetic magic that turned on the word *lock*. So the Side Door by association became My Door. In the most intimate terms, it 'spoke to my blood'. That is how I thought of it. When Our Burglar chose just this door to break in by I was deeply disturbed. Might there be something sympathetic in that as well?

The world is full of odd, undisclosed connections. Our house was alive with them. But none seemed odder, or more alarming and secret, than the one I felt between my nose, the key to the Side Door and that faceless intruder, the Young Fellow in sandshoes who had been in our house for no more than a quarter of an hour perhaps but had smelled out, in that time, even in darkness, more of its connecting paths than I had in a lifetime. Do burglars, I wondered, have some sixth sense that allows them to see the threads between things as a luminous net? If so, then what I really wanted to be when I grew up was not a fireman or a famous surgeon but a burglar. That is why I needed to see our burglar's face, to sit down and have a good chinwag with him. The Side Door was the connection between us. When Cassie slipped its key down my back a cold shiver went through me. My blood stopped.

But all this is body talk, and I see now that I tune my ears and listen to it – or rather, now that I recall in an active manner my nose – that I have omitted something from my description of our Front Room that was the real reason for going back to it. Memory has played a trick on me. One of my senses has declined to work. How else have my nostrils failed to detect, among the mingled odours of dusty velvet, furniture polish, Brasso and the damp of ancient floorboards, a smell that is different in kind from the rest, a familiar, not unpleasant odour that cuts clean through the metal and cloth and wood-smells, and brings to this overfurnished garden the authentic odour of shit. For there, in a hidden corner, on the polished forest-floor, is a pile of turds. It is my habit to bless, in this direct and simple manner, certain places in the house that are my particular concern. (Have I been reminded of this by my evocation of Our Burglar, and the habit of some housebreakers – animal, childish, primitive – of leaving such 'signatures' in the houses they have robbed?)

I am punished for the offence but I persist. These are gift-offerings. I leave them in special places. Perhaps they are cold spots in the house that need, I feel, to be heated by this easy expression of my body's warmth, or dangerous places I want to leave my scent on and appease. I am speaking with what is, for the time being, my body's only expressive mouth, poems that are hymns or critical protests – who knows which? Whatever I intend, it is in a particular corner of our Front Room, the forbidden garden of delights, that I choose most often to leave this evidence of myself, and what I have done, in the peculiar argot of the household, is a *job*. (I am amused at the attempt to find a place for this low natural function in the 'work ethic', and the suggestion, all confused as it is in my mind with burglary, of a vocation. This body talk, which seems so local, opens into a real social world. So I am invited to speak of my penis, back there – with what appeal to aggression and lawlessness? – as my *trigger*.)

And so at last we come down to it, the body – that small hot engine at the centre of all these records and recollections; gravely preoccupied, as it hoovers about the house and yard, with its own business of breathing, pumping blood, processing the fruits of the earth, but in every sense meeting reality head on – as dirt that stains, sunshine that warms or burns, berries that delight the eye but when tasted catch fire in the mouth. And is that smell lemon-blossom or some passing woman's scent?

The world is all edges. They bruise for a time, drawing to the surface of the skin a purple storm-cloud than can be seen but not heard, no matter how hard you strain your ear. There are raw nails, open chocolate-boxes, the glass panes of louvres that in a single, sharp encounter will leave this body marked with a pit in the softness of the calf and a ridge of hard scar-tissue across the kneecap; on the ball of the thumb a puffy mound with stitch marks (a butcher's job).

It is out of the hot core of this body, its constant heat, that I test the climate of the world, its cool places, its dead cold ones. It is from a changing height as my eyes move about in it, two feet seven one year, three feet two the next, as the door to the Piano Room would show, that I judge dimensions, including my own, and the distance at which I stand from things.

A complex assembly: of organs, nerve-ends, bones, cartilage, muscle. An experience machine, that observes, thinks, smells, attends, touches. It learns to listen in this forest for the creaking of familiar boards that is the approach of this or that sharer of the house, and as the day's heat ebbs and the old house-frame resettles, marks the distance we have moved into night. It gets cramps and growing-pains; it sweats, stinks, grumbles; but at certain intangible contacts, it soars till it might be angelic, gifted with unique, undeniable powers – of flight, of change, of eternal instant being. It is always in a state becoming. Only in the last and most private room of all do we come upon it – not still, not fully revealed, but alone, unguarded, and in easy nakedness.

[VII]

You enter the Bathroom up one step from what we call the Kitchen, a long room divided by an archway like the one in the Hall, only grander; a wooden arc springing from fluted pedestals and with leaded glass in the frames – pink, mauve and crimson flowers of a kind that do not exist in nature but which respond to it just the same. They glow or are muted according to the weather and change every hour of the day.

The larger section is our dining-room. The smaller, beyond the arch, is Cassie's cooking and washing-up place. Here, on an Early Kooka gas-stove with a laughing jackass on the front, she prepares the enormous meals of those days, meals that defy latitude and the facts of climate and weather by reproducing the baked dinners, stews, hot-pots and boiled puddings of the Mother Country (our mother's country), which we continue to consume, after more than a century, as if a hundred degrees of humidity constituted a strictly moral challenge, and we had our real existence in a cold place on the other side of the globe. Physical bodies and the actual have nothing to do with it. In a properly British way we ignore them, as we ignore the view from the window on to a backyard that dazzles in sunlight, steams after rain, and is choked with tropical weeds out of which cannas burst in scarlet and golden flames.

What we are feeding when, at fixed hours – breakfast at seven, dinner at noon, tea at six-thirty – we assemble behind serviette-rings initialled with our names, are the spirits of the fathers. We are paying tribute to origins – even those of us whose origins are of another kind.

So we sweat and consume: Steak and Kidney Pudding, Rolled Shoulder of Lamb with Mint Sauce and Potatoes Carrots and Peas, Roast Beef and Yorkshire Pudding, Corned Beef with Cauliflower and White Sauce, all washed down with tea and followed by one of the sweet puddings that on hot afternoons blow steam out under the lid of an aluminium saucepan as they boil the hours away in a cloth or in a special pudding-basin with a clip-over top: Sago Plum-Pudding, Ginger Pudding, Golden Syrup Pudding, Spotted Dick.

It is a distinguishably different body, then, that goes up that one step into the old-fashioned bathroom and strips itself to view, a body fed with different notions of itself as well as different food. For our bodies are inventions; we shape them to our views. This contemporary body we move in, which seems to belong so deeply to the world of nature, is a work of art, the product of convention, fashion, diet – of pure idea and the power of advertising. The body of forty years ago, though anatomically the same, will show, when we observe it closely, a subtle difference. It is, as we see from its roughness and scars, less cared for than our modern one, less conscious of itself and of some ideal beauty to which it might be expected to conform; or the ideal is of another kind.

Women's bodies are chunkier, their legs plumper than might be acceptable now, particularly at the knee. Largely undieted, they are constrained by a girdle and have one shape when they are attired and a quite different one when they are not. In the soft flesh at the top of the thigh there is the impression of suspender-belt buttons.

It is a body that retains its hair and is not deodorised. In repose it sags, and the emphasis is less on good lines, good bones, than on the roundness of the flesh. Even without the clothes that distinguish one decade from the next, it is a body of the past. There is a lingering memory of the classical about it, of the Renaissance, the Nineties. And if men's bodies seem more familiar, and less easy therefore to date, it is because they, save for an inch or two of average growth, have undergone fewer transformations, or because the ideal in their case is not the product of aesthetic fantasy but of physical hard work, and those forms of play that are hard work disciplined and refined.

The rooms that serve these bodies reflect them. Modern bathrooms are secular shrines. Under lights as brilliant as in any theatre, the body is apotheosised, becomes a stage for all those evolutionary disciplines that create the godlike creature, all its human imperfections smoothed and disguised, that TV advertisements sing extravagant hymns to and heated towel rails, a vanity, a cubicle devoted entirely to the rituals of the shower, ferns, goldfish, a cane chair or two and a battery of sockets for shavers, vibrators, toothbrushes and hair-driers, are called from all corners of the earth to mollify and make fine. This is a holy of holies. Here household gods are present in the flesh.

Old-style bathrooms (of which ours was entirely typical) were the product of a simpler and poorer economy and served a body with simpler needs.

Stripped to the bare essentials, and with all their functions rudely undisguised, they were not intended or furnished for the pursuit of the ideal, or for uncovering erotic possibilities, or ministering alone or in company to the flesh. What you practised before their brutal plumbing and beaten-tin walls, in a spirit of dour austerity, was the virtue that was next to godliness; and it was most nearly a virtue when you did not linger over it. You did what you had to do briskly, efficiently, and you never locked the door.

The bath is of enamelled iron. It stands high on clawed feet, with a cold tap at one end and a geyser at the other. The geyser roars when lighted. In it, as in the bath, some animal form has been reduced to metal and crudely stylised – reminder of a continuity to which we also belong. After a few unroyal splutters it emits a trickle of steam.

Overhead a galvanised-iron shower, with a rose so large, and with such wide perforations, that it might better, I think, be called a sunflower. A bathmat of wooden slats, water-softened and worn at the centre. The towel-rail also wood. The only other furnishings a linen-press where fresh towels are kept and a little two-shelved medicine-chest, high up out of reach; and on the wall opposite, a full-length mirror with a kitchen chair in front, where we stand to be dried after our bath and to have our hair combed when we are going out.

The mirror seems out of place. It is too grand for here. It has a metal frame that might once have been bronze, its egg-and-dart pattern subdued but not quite extinguished with paint. Too large for mere convenience – shaving for example – it might encourage illusions of a baroque sort if our imaginations could jump to them. Standing in front of it you see: black-and-white-checked lino in big squares like the chessboard in

Musgrave Park, a lion's paw, the geyser, and the passage that leads to our lavatory.

There is no wash-stand or basin. We wash our face and hands over the bath, with cold water and Lifebuoy soap; but the soap-holder, galvanised iron in which my father has punched irregular holes for drainage, contains as well a pumice stone, a scratchy loofah and the bar of abrasive Solvol with which he scrubs up after a day in the toolshed or mowing the lawn. Our hair we wash in rainwater out in the yard, in a basin by the watertank, with a jug for rinsing.

Between the linen-press and the bath is another door. It opens into a passage, a no-man's-land with no source of light and no electric light of its own between the Bathroom proper and our cubby-hole of a lavatory. Here, at the bottom of a cupboard whose shelves are crammed with all sorts of broken stuff and rubbish – old *Photoplays* and pattern books, oil-lamps, meat-dishes and boxes of discoloured snapshots – are our bulk provisions: sugar, salt and rice in hundredweight sacks, string bags bulging with potatoes and onions.

It is a creepy, half-way place, only partly domesticated. There are cockroaches. You can hear them scuttling about when the bathwater shuts off. And rats. Our father has laid pink and white baits he gets from the Council, little squares of poisonous coconut-ice. So the book when I discover it, with its evocation of a dark, half-animal world, does not seem surprising or out of place.

I have been locked in for an hour, because my sister and I have been scrapping, and decide to amuse myself from the cupboard shelves. It is light enough. The mice keep out of sight if you scrape your shoes a little, and I am used to cockroaches.

I find first of all some old snapshots, several of which I already know. One is of my parents on a picnic at Peel Island – 'where the lepers were'. In another they are standing knee-deep in the surf at Coolangatta, and my father is holding me, aged seven or eight months, in his arms. A big wave is coming and my father is holding me out to it. I have my mouth open, screaming. I am learning not to be afraid of the sea. But today, feeling bolder than usual, I go deeper. Pushed down behind a stack of broken soup tureens I find a book.

I like books. This one is small, about the same size as a prayer book, only thicker, and with a cover the cockroaches have eaten: red but blotched now with white. It has pictures, and they are of a kind I have never encountered before, crudely printed in black ink.

One of them is a sheep-child, a little boy with the face and chest of a human but the woolly body and feet of a lamb. Another is a dog-boy. Fiercer. There is nothing frightening about these creatures. They are odd, that's all. I think them wonderful. They give me such a marvellous sense of possibilities, of how the world of animals and men might be connected. It is only when I sit down to read the text that I become alarmed. Here are deep warnings to women against having to do with sheep, dogs, asses (or lions and tigers, it might be) and against exposing themselves, while with child, to any deformity. A woman, it seems, might produce one of these children by being frightened by a passing dog.

I close the book and push it back (and used to think of it later with real excitement, hidden away with its 'secrets').

So creation contains more than the colouring books let on. Giraffes, hippos, whales, for all their oddness, I accept and believe in, though I have never actually seen one. Now sheep-boys! But where are they? Do their parents hide them away?

I go back into the bathroom, and with no particular sense of anxiety, in a spirit of pure curiosity, take all my clothes off, climb onto the chair and stand staring at my small naked body in the glass. It is the first time I have ever really looked at myself. There is no sign of hair.

But when Cassie comes in and finds me there I am punished a second time and sent to exile in the yard. Where I go and help Grandpa stake some tomato plants, then watch the rooster among our chooks.

The body has two lives as it has two sides, an outward and visible one and a dark, interior life that follows laws and processes we cannot always control. The life of the inner body is obscure, and the rooms that are set aside to serve it share that obscurity, more in some places and at some times than others, and even when they are clearly to be seen.

Brisbane lavatories at the time of which I am writing are still set at a distance, outside at the bottom of the yard. Weather-board dunnies with a corrugated-iron roof swathed with bougainvillaea or a loaded choko vine, they are serviced by a night-man; when you shut the door you are in the dark. Our lavatory, in fact, has been brought inside but has brought the dark in with it. At the end of the storeroom passageway, behind a three-ply screen with no door, you sit in utter blackness on a split-seated throne that pinches. Berries drop into the guttering overhead. Warm air gusts up through the floorboards from under-the-house.

Our cubbyhole of a lavatory is one exit into the body's dark. There is another. High up on the Bathroom wall is a door of doll's house size and the only one here that is securely latched. Beyond it, the smallest room of all. When you open the door and look into its white-painted interior you are looking into the body's dark places. When you approach it you are stepping through into another age. Lined up on its two narrow shelves are the patent and homemade remedies that in those days, before antibiotics and the arrival of the big drug companies, constitute our entire armoury against the body's ills, and what their paucity reveals is how little can be done before the body ceases to be close and treatable and moves into that slide area where the powers of medicine shockingly fail. Parents live in a state of permanent anxiety; and children, while suffering easily enough the nicks, jabs and scars of rough play in a world of edges, unconcerned as all children are by the future disadvantages of a gouge under the left eye, or stitches or a dead tooth, are aware just the same, through endless warnings, of lockjaw, blood poisoning, polio, even hydrophobia as we called it then – all runaway illnesses that represent the irruption into the body of a chaos beyond control.

The body that stands in this relation to a rose thorn or a splinter stands in a different relation to nature as a whole, belongs to an age as remote in its way as that gothic world in which lepers shook their bells in dark alleys and men danced themselves to death with St Anthony's fire. It is the age before penicillin.

So there it is on two shelves: a bottle of peroxide for applying to spots, warts, whitlows and for removing green from the teeth; a bottle of Solyptol, a few drops of which, as a general protection, go into the bath (it clouds the water like Pernod) and is applied neat to barked shins, grazed knees and cat bites; an embrocation of my father's own recipe, made up from oil of eucalyptus and metho; a roll of cotton-wool, a roll of lint, a roll of elastoplast; a tin of Goanna Salve (native cure-all); chocolate Laxettes for children and Agarol for the adults; milk of magnesia, castor-oil, cod-liver oil and malt, and a can of antiphlogestine paste to be boiled, spread on lint and slapped scalding on to the chest. These remedies, which belong as much, some of them, to folk myth as to medicine, go back to my parents' childhood, and beyond that even into the previous century.

But it isn't simply another time we are dealing with now, another era; or even, in purely physical terms, another body differently treated. It is a body differently conceived of, differently seen; and the truth is that for all ordinary purposes it is barely seen at all. Full, self-consciousness nakedness is a condition so rare as to be perverse.

Contemporary bodies walk naked, even when they are fully clothed. You see that in the ease with which they present themselves. But the owners of these earlier bodies have no sense of their own nakedness. The body is at a distance behind intricate fastenings, under layer on layer of cloth. Women wear petticoats, panties and corsets of a pink stuff stiffened with bone, a strip of which occasionally protrudes like a secret rib; the lacing is that of an elongated shoe. Even trousers have a system of braces and flybuttons that are not easily negotiated, and undershorts are buttoned not elasticated. It takes time to get into the 'nuddy' – a word that is intended to suggest the comic nature of the event, to strip it of eroticism. Nakedness is a condition that even the mind cannot arrive at till it has dealt with an array of inhibiting braces and buttons and straps.

So the body, back there, that stands naked before a glass, having laid aside corsets, spencer, swami-silk panties and lisle stockings (or flannel trousers, singlet and knee-length shorts) has arrived at a different nakedness and by another and slower route. It is a body that accepts itself as imperfect. It has odours and body-hair, shows scars that scarcely matter since they are in places that will never be revealed. It is a sensuous body; all those buttons, straps and laces, those odours, even the scars, constitute a possible and powerful eroticism; *but* –

And here we come to a limit. That *but* is a threshold we cannot cross, since even if we could find the door to that room, we cannot now find in ourselves the body, the experiencing mind-in-the-body, to go through. That body is out of reach. And it isn't simply a matter of its being forgotten in us – of a failure of memory or imagination to summon it up, but of a change in perceiving itself. What moving back into it would demand is an act of *un*-remembering, a dismantling of the body's experience that would be a kind of dying, a casting off, one by one, of all the tissues of perception, conscious and not, through which our very notion of body has been remade. We would have to give back to oblivion the antibodies and complex immunity systems that for nearly four decades now have freed us into a lighter being, a safer and more biddable nature; remove from our blood the knowledge it has acquired from all those smokes and acids that, in changing the body's awareness of reality, have changed *it*. We would have to cleanse our skin of its contact with nylon and acrylic, and tease out of our sense of how modern buildings smell the sharp, unmistakable odour given off by all those objects and utensils that are made of plastic – toothbrush handles, price tags, the tags on new-born babies' wrists, waste disposal bags, icecream cartons, toy cars and watches, combs, transfusion drips. We would have to darken on our palate the light of new foods, avocado, muesli, yoghurt, and shake off from our limbs the dance steps, Rock n' Roll and the Twist, that have taught us a new way of moving. We would have to empty ourselves of the experience of travelling up a lift shaft at twenty-five storeys per second, and the power we feel (to cover distances, to eat up the world) when we are projected horizontally at seven hundred miles an hour over the curve of the earth. Most of all, we would have to step out of the body that has been born in us under the touch (on parts of the old one we barely knew existed) of hands, mouths, tongues – a creature stranger than any sheep-child, and only shyly emergent, but eager already to explore the universe. It has been formed in us by the reorganisation of all the parts of our body in a new order, where mouth for example, after its long re-creation of itself as a speaking organ, has become a finger-pad to test the subtlest texture of things, a third eye for seeing colours the rainbow missed, sighting new horizons –

A limit. A wall we cannot go through. Which is in some ways where we began. Except that memory, in leading us back, has turned us about. It has drawn us through room after room towards a past body, an experience of the world that cannot be entered, only to confront us with a future body that can. Memory is deeper than we are and has longer views. When it pricked and set us on, it was the future it had in mind, and the door our fingertips were seeking was not there because we were looking in the wrong place; it was not that door we were meant to go through. The door was in us. Our actual body is the wall our fingertips come to. We have only to dare one last little blaze of magic to pass through.

A Place in Tuscany

[1]

Early maps show C. as a walled rectangular town laid out along the line of the ridge, with square towers projecting at every fifty metres and the parish church, *la Pieve*, at the summit.

All the towns in this area sit on high hills. When the Romans left, and their irrigation systems fell into disuse, the great plain of the Maremma reverted to marshy, malarial country, famous like the Camargue for its horses but fatal to men. Exile to the Maremma was used by the Medici and the later Grand Dukes of Tuscany as a delayed death sentence. The place has remained half wild. Cork woods and wild boar abound; ancient cattle of enormous size, and tough squat cowboys are still to be seen in the dune country towards the mouth of the Ombrone; settlements, most of them going back to Etruscan times, are scattered.

C. was once the most important town in the area and is still the centre of a *Comune*. Most of its walls survive and the houses are built into them. Their thickness can be gauged by the low tunnel-shaped entries that are still in use on the south-west side, where a line of towers, all perfectly intact, look across the plain to the sea. They have long sloping steps, beamed ceilings, and measure six metres from one level to the next. The last of the towers has been converted to a belfry. All summer an intense, half-witted boy who has constituted himself the town firewatcher sits up there with a walkie-talkie set, scanning the plain for flames.

A vast jigsaw of spaces that fit one into another, the village piles century on century and is still in the process of being made. Built of a mixture of granite boulders and tufa, it is grim in winter, but when the stone is touched with sunlight it mellows to a soft gold. Roofs are flat and projecting, and are of corrugated terracotta, blotched with grey-green or yellow lichen and held down against the wind with stones. Every house has dark-green slatted shutters, long windows with varnished frames and inner shutters of solid white. Under each window are rings for flowerpots and a smaller ring for a flag.

One side of the village faces north-east into the wild country towards Siena. It gets no sun after mid-morning and bears the full blast in winter of the *tramontana*. The other faces the sea. Protected from chill winds, it gets the sun in winter, the sea breeze at five o'clock every summer evening and on clear days the sea itself is a glowing band between the hills. It appears so suddenly at times, when the late sun strikes it, as to make a flash at the corner of my eye as I sit working, as if out there somewhere a match had been struck.

At such times the whole plain comes alive in all its detail of fields, pasture, vineyards, olive groves, and the mountains as ridge after ridge of impenetrable *macchia*.

What are the characteristic sights of this landscape?

In high summer, when the earth is baked hard and everything is yellow-brown after the harvest, gabled 'houses', sometimes fifty metres long, appear in the fields. They look like primitive temples and are made of great blocks of hay. Other fields are lined with the giant mill-wheels turned out by another brand of harvester. Only small land-holders make hay in the old way, as a round stack with a conical roof, that is gradually sliced away till it resembles a waisted hourglass.

Very strange they look in late summer moonlight, these impermanent structures – megalithic temples, mill-wheels, hourglasses in the flat fields.

In autumn, when the hills have been ploughed and show their original colours from blond, through all the ochres to black, the strangest sight here, especially on days of frost, is the bare-boughed persimmon with its orange fruit, each one more brilliant than the sun. They look sinister; like witches' apples, turning transparent as they ripen and rot. Below them, chrysanthemums – white, yellow, pink, rust. They are grown here not as house-flowers, but to be carried, first at All Souls, then each Sunday afterwards, to the cemetery, where every grave has its pot. These are the extravagant, abundant, wonderfully fleshy and long-lasting flowers of the dead.

Spring. Elaborately dressed plastic dolls appear in the boughs of cherry trees, all bows and bonnets like hanged babies. They are meant to scare off birds.

In May, great swarms of fireflies, in such brilliant drifts that on moonless nights you can see your way by them. Nightingales. And from the vineyards the regular boom of the automatic cannon that are used to keep off boar. All night they go boom boom. In poorer vineyards, sleepy children beat saucepans, and all the way into the distance the dogs bark.

Easy to see here how a cuisine comes into existence. It has nothing to do with the refinements of art.

For one whole month there are only artichokes and broad

beans; in another tomatoes, runner-beans, zucchini; cherries till you cannot bear the sight of them; later strawberries. Everyone has a brief surplus of everything, to be eaten, given away, pickled, or dried and preserved under oil. There are no luxuries. A luxury is an ordinary commodity available at the wrong time or in the wrong place. Here everything is ordinary and has, prepared in as many different ways as possible, to be eaten till it is used up and the next thing appears. Cuisine makes the necessary palatable.

Every family here eats out of its own *orto* – seldom bigger than the kitchen, often the size of a kitchen table – where half a dozen artichokes, a row of broad beans, lettuce, tomato, and various kinds of spinach keep a household going throughout the year. Basil and sage grow on windowsills, capers in the crevices of walls, and rosemary, with its pretty blue flower, in unruly six-foot hedges.

All of this speaks for the abundance but also the frugality of Tuscan living. Nothing is wasted. Mealtimes are serious social occasions, prolonged and formal both in shape and in the rituals they follow, but the fare is simple, healthy, boring; coarse unsalted bread is the staple, oil instead of butter, and everything is cooked on top of the stove. My friend Agatina, I notice, uses her oven for storing crockery, and when it is empty and open the cats sleep there.

When I acquired Agatina's house (as it is still called in the village) I also acquired Agatina, her husband, Ugo, eighty-two, and her sister, Celeste, who died last month at eighty-six. I go to Sunday lunch and sometimes in the late afternoon as well, to sit in the kitchen with the women; drinking sweet tea, watching them do their needlework, and listening to Agatina's stories. Over the years I have also acquired the history of this family of intelligent, well-to-do *contadini* (our word, peasant, won't quite do) who own several houses in the village and many small pieces of land with olives, vines, cherries and figs.

Agatina's parents and all four of her brothers and sisters once lived in my house. The father, who was lazy and fond of drink, died of a fall at the bottom of my inner staircase; Agatina never fails to sigh over the spot and to warn me against coming down in the dark. (She is too polite to mention drunkenness.)

Her mother, during the six days in which the Germans occupied the village at the end of the war, including the thirty-six hours of the actual battle, sat quietly in a kind of priest's hole under my bathroom. Celeste sat in the fireplace above. She refused to flee, or to hide like the other villagers in the *macchia*. Quite un-intimidated by bombardments and falling shells she stayed to defend the family linen. I imagine her sitting upright in the great chimney-place, all in black (she had worn mourning since the death of a favourite brother in the Great War) and imagine her conversations with the old lady below. She must have been in her middle forties then. I have seen photographs of her as an elegant woman of thirty-five or so, sitting in a cane chair beside the sea. Until quite recently she was alert, upright, lucid – she knew the birthdate of every man, woman and child in the village, you had only to mention the name and she would produce it – not at all fierce like Agatina, but with great authority. The family linen, needless to say, was saved.

She never married. As the eldest daughter she brought up all the younger children, and when she died in her sleep recently, after feeling less well than usual, Agatina felt she had lost a mother more than a sister. Celeste, she affirms, was a saint, and Agatina, who is punctiliously observant but not really pious, is furious with God for having taken her. She had asked as a special grace that Celeste should live to ninety and had already bought the candles. For three days during a hot spell she refused to believe that the grace would not be extended.

Agatina, as she would be the first to admit, is not saintlike. Very small and powerfully plain, she is bossy, bad-tempered, humorous, shrewd, a passionate defender of family and of all friends, and in the village much respected and feared.

Her husband, Ugo, comes from a rival place on the other side of the valley. Very tall and handsome, an ex-gamekeeper, he is entirely his own man, but inside the house Agatina rules. He is paid the traditional deference of being asked whether the *pasta* is cooked, and is always served first: but he suffers, I think, from being an outsider and from having married above himself; Agatina still uses, as many local women do, her family name. The house, both in fact and spirit, is hers. Only in these last days, when he has been too weak to go into the fields, has Ugo ever spent time in the big kitchen, which is the one room of the house in general use. It is sad to see him sitting on a little chair by the window with his stick in his hand and the three cats at his feet.

The kitchen in these houses is the women's room; men, if they are not eating or sleeping, are expected to be either in the fields or at the bar. It is the largest and warmest room in the house. Here the television stands, playing all through every mealtime – an awesome experience at Agatina's since, as she often says, 'two of the three people in this house, and one of the cats, are stone deaf'. Here too, the women gather at the kitchen table, which is spread between meals with a good lace cloth, to gossip, knit, or do their elaborate fancy-work – Agatina with a little wooden footstool because her feet do not reach the floor. This footstool is a relic of the days when, in my tiny sitting-room, she made her living by minding children, thirty at a time, while their mothers were in the fields. It is of thick walnut, about nine inches long and six high, and belonged, forty years ago, to an orphan, now the husband of her favourite niece.

Such details, and many more, Agatina has passed on to me with the absolute assurance that as a writer I will be interested and may one day 'set it down'. I know now almost every significant event in her life.

The oldest brother, Baldo (Garibaldo), died heroically in the Alps in 1917. He was killed taking rations to a group of his comrades who were isolated under bombardment on a nearby hill, and Agatina tells the story in the high rhetoric these people reserve for such occasions, and in a language, very close to Dante's, that has all the flourishes, and tenses, of high literary art.

Baldo had asked an officer if the men on the hill were not to have their rations. Impossible, the officer replied. What, said Baldo, are our comrades to die of hunger as well as from the enemy guns? Are we to stand by and suffer this shame? With that he loaded a mule, set off, delivered the rations, and was killed on the way down. He was just twenty-four. I have seen – one of the treasures in a little museum of photographs and other mementos under the oil-cloth of Agatina's kitchen table – a letter from this youth to the parents of a fallen friend. Beautifully penned, in the most correct and eloquent Italian, it is full of high feeling and heroic affirmations of patriotism and revenge, and ends with a poem.

Baldo, who had no formal education beyond fifteen, wrote many such letters. He regarded it as his duty. After the war in 1919, Agatina's uncle, the priest, used these letters to prepare a history of the village fallen and the circumstances of their deaths. It is a slim book, impressive as these things always are, printed at Poggibonsi in a pale green cover with art nouveau lilies. It is called Flowers and Tears. Baldo, in Agatina's kitchen, after nearly seventy years, is most marvellously alive.

But all the dead are still living here. They are living in the *campo santo* beyond the church, a large walled area, a rectangle very like the one C. itself makes on ancient maps, with its own chapels and funerary monuments and a great wall of slabs, each with an electric candle. The whole place glows at night like an alternative village, which is what it is; a neighbouring, utterly ordinary and unfrightening 'village of the dead'. Sunday visits are made there; there is continuous traffic on the road.

Death here is a commonplace and sociable occurrence. Black-edged notices appear in the square beside the daily headlines. The bell tolls – a single long stroke for a man, a two-note broken one for a woman. Everyone hears and knows.

But if not shocking, or even shameful as it sometimes is with us, death always comes unexpectedly and too soon. She was only eighty-six, Agatina says of Celeste, why her? There are others so much older. (It is true: half the village seems to be over eighty.) She wasn't *old*.

Once, when I had a fever, Agatina came and insisted that I call a doctor. These fevers, she told me, are dangerous. There was a girl here died of such a fever last week. Terrible! Absolutely overnight. Which girl? I asked. You know her – Carlina. Died overnight. But Agatina, I protested, she was eighty-three! Precisely. So you see you can't be too careful. Call the doctor and make sure he gives you a suppository. (Italians are addicted to all sorts of drugs and the pharmacy in any village is a wonder of wonders. But suppositories are, for quite primitive reasons I suspect, the favourite of all remedies, and indispensable to any serious cure.)

Sunday at Agatina's: In the summer, when the clock has been put forward, we eat early enough for our meal to coincide with the Pope's mass on television.

Time in Agatina's house is a sacred commodity, not to be interfered with. She despises the 'legal' hour. All her clocks keep the real one, and she felt magnificently justified last year when a workman (*poveretto!*) fell to his death in a nearby village while changing the hands of the clock.

So all through lunch in summer we eat with the Pope's Mass at full volume, and Celeste and Agatina, between sips of soup and bursts of gossip, participate in all the responses, spoken and sung.

'That Eglantina, I tell you, is a perfect viper – Hear us O Lord,' says Agatina. 'This pasta is not my best,' says Celeste. 'I apologise, *Professore* – Hallelujah, hallelujah, blessed be he who comes.' The three cats, which climb over the backs of our chairs and leap up to sniff at saucepans, are driven off with swipes and a holy, holy, holy. Papa Woytila's health is commented on from week to week: 'He looks worse – he's failing. And he's not even sixty!'

Mass is followed by the news bulletin with its lists of newly arrested terrorists and the death-toll in the gang wars in Naples (357 since the beginning of the year) and Palermo (116). It all seems very distant, like news from another country or from a century we have not yet reached.

It is. Italy is a misty, metaphysical concept here. 'Look at that cat,' says Agatina, 'she understands every word! Just like a Christian.' She means just like a human being. On another occasion, when I have brought, say, a Dutchman and two Australians to see her, she will say, 'Oh well, we're all Italians here.' She is speaking of our common humanity.

The truth is that the village is its own world, as complete and self-enclosed, even without its walls, as it was 100 or 900 years ago. Its months are measured by the work that is appropriate to them, as in old sculptures: ploughing and harrowing, seeding, harvesting, grape-picking, the olives; and its years by who was born there. 'I am from '96,' Celeste would say, reckoning in the Italian manner. Time is concrete or it has no meaning. The dead go on forever in a new place at the bottom of the hill and their lights burn long after the village itself goes dark. As for geography, that gives out at the first horizon.

'Australia,' Agatina says, as she might say Saturn or Paradise. It is a continent she has now acquired, in the sense in which I have acquired her family history; she locates it in some empty area of her experience between Poland, where Papa Woytila comes from, and New York, where a grand-niece recently spent the summer. It is the place I exist in, in her thoughts, when I am not fifty metres away in 'her' house. Time is too continuous, too present, too large to be thought about, and space too small. Such are the conditions of this world!

[11]

Wednesday, January 9

When I got up this morning, just before eight, the window-panes were thickly coated with frost. It was only when I scratched a little of it away with my fingernail and peered through that I saw the whole countryside was white and the low wall of Agatina's garden, and the roof of the house opposite, were frosted with inches of soft, new-fallen snow. No sign of the sun. The sky was white, low, opaque, suffused with light of a kind I have never seen in this part of the country – unearthly. When the snow started up again, just on ten, at first in tiny granules, then in great fat flakes, the sky took on a more familiar hue and one felt a kind of relief that what had begun to fall was, after all, just snow.

The village is in a state of silly excitement. There is no school, no one has gone to work. The last time snow fell to this depth was in 1929, and when I call at Agatina's they can all, of course, recall the occasion, even Agatina's nephew Baldo who would have been six or seven years old. They seem delighted, as if two parts of their life have made contact again over a great distance, as if 1929, all those years back before the war, had been revived, made real again, confirming their existence in time and re-establishing even more firmly their presence now. Baldo, the nephew, in Russian-style fur hat with ear-flaps and fur-collared jacket, is six years old again. He sits on the high bread-box, swinging his feet.

Agatina, even more skittish than usual, gives me a wink. She raises her apron and three black skirts to show what is under her chair: a little copper bucket full of coals. When she gets up she takes it with her to warm her hands. She is about to make polenta (*polenda* she calls it), traditional cold-weather food, and insists that I come back to eat with them at noon. Well, for this once I shall. As she takes down the big bronze cooking-pot she enquires about my visitors. Do I still think they will come? She shakes her head. No, *Professore*, impossible! The road up from the highway is all ice, no one can get in or out of the village. Even the *Rama*, the bus from Grosseto, has failed to get through. The autostrada between Florence and Bologna is piled up with abandoned vehicles – the overnight temperature there was twenty below. They won't come.

This is the opinion too of Giuseppina at our little supermarket when I go to lay in provisions, just in case, and of Eidé at the Post Office where I enquire if there has, perhaps, been a telegram. They won't get through. Still, I prepare a casserole of sausages and beans, and about three in the afternoon go out with a shovel and spend a bitter half-hour clearing the steps, sweeping hard with a broom so that there is no chance of thin ice forming. My hands freeze. The temperature is eleven below.

It is unnaturally quiet. All day no car has passed the house, either in my own narrow street or on the road below. The only sound is of young people, boys mostly but sometimes one of the rowdier girls as well, engaging in skirmishes with snowballs or rolling one another over in the soft snow.

It snows again at four. I keep the stove fed with logs, read a little, finally at half-past seven make myself an omelette. Then at eight there is the sound of a car, just the motor. It can only be them. And sure enough, a big Volvo station-wagon has pulled up just past my steps, and Richard Tipping, hatless in the red glow of the rear lamps, is in the street below, shouting 'Here, it must be here.'

They have come all the way from Milan without chains. The driver, a thick-set, round-faced fellow, all smiles, is a cross-country motor-bike rider – all this to him is child's play. Anyway, they've made it, they're here. I am introduced and they begin to bring in their equipment: great blue canvas bags, tripods, screens, clipped aluminium boxes in several sizes. They soon make a pile four feet high in the corner of my kitchen.

I am impressed at the speed with which Richard has set all this up. In just three weeks, in a foreign country and with Christmas and New Year between, he has found all this equipment, got finance, insurance, gathered a crew.

Bob Shaffer, the cameraman, is an American, working freelance wherever he can but based in Milan. He has just flown in from Morocco, where he has been working on a film about the American writer, Paul Bowles. He is off next to New York to make a film about transvestites.

Alex, the driver, is his sound engineer, and a third fellow is on the way from Rome; they have to go in and pick him up at Grosseto off the Rome–Genoa *rapido*. He is Bob's assistant, Adriano, who will go to New York with him on the transvestites job but is working on our film for the love of it, because if there's a film to be made he wants to be in on it.

We decide to eat later, when we are all assembled, and I put the casserole on again. But first we must go up to my friend Joan's house at Poggio Madonna, half a kilometre away, to regulate the heating in the little guest flat she has lent me, where two of the crew will sleep. Then Bob and Alex will drive in to Grosseto while Richard and I look through the notes he has made of what I shall read. These matters have to be settled tonight. First thing in the morning we will get out and start shooting. We have just two days.

There is, as yet, no script. Richard and I both have shapes in our heads, different ones no doubt, but they are adaptable; they must be. All this snow for example was not provided for when we began, but here it is. It will obviously be a major factor now. I see it as a metaphor for the snowbound state of isolation I am in when I am shut up here in the village, with no telephone, no car, absorbed in a book. It is as if I had produced it, by magic or a free act of the imagination, to make my point. Anyway, wherever it has come from, it is now a fact and will impose its own conditions. When we go out in it, it will determine what we can do, how we do it and play its own part in the thing. So that is 'the script'. Only what I read can be fixed.

At half-past ten, with Bob and Alex still not back from Grosseto (the *rapido* was expected at nine), Richard and I go down to Trento's bar, the Bar Hawaii, so that he can call his wife.

Trento's is a long gloomy place with a bar on the left, billiards tables downstairs, a little enclosed phone-box where you escape into hermetic silence, and windows at the end that open – except that they are barred now – on to a high and distant view.

The bar is hot tonight. All the little tables are crowded with card-players, almost invisible in a fog of breath and thick smoke. They slap their cards down hard, shouting 'Briscola!' Near the entrance, half a dozen village kids, some of them not much more than eight years old, are playing computer football, working their arms furiously and cheering on their teams.

Busy preparations are being made. Out in the square several boys and young men, all wrapped up in coloured scarves and wearing snow-boots, are about to ski to the highway – a downhill run of five kilometres. Others will take the back road to the Ombrone.

It is a bright clear night, fiercely cold. The new snow shines. We troop out with others to see the start. They set off, fifteen or twenty of them, down the deserted main street of the village and out of sight round the corner, followed by cars fitted with chains to bring them up again.

Midnight. We are assembled. We sit down at last to eat.

Thursday, January 10

Nine o'clock. After a good breakfast we go down, all four, to take a walk round the village and see what we might film. But as soon as he sees the light, Bob decides we should make the most of it and start shooting immediately.

It is cold but brilliantly clear, and all this side of the village is bathed in golden sunlight.

While we set off uphill, Alex the sound man is to go down into the village and make recordings. He wears a hip-length anorak, khaki with a fur-lined hood, and snowboots. Strapped to his side is the rectangular recorder, and he carries a flexible sound-rod with a spongy microphone, a little bigger than a tennis-ball, hanging from the end of it. With the hood drawn over his face, which is lost in the circlet of fur, and his short stocky build, he looks like an Eskimo, or a space walker putting his feet down carefully, awkwardly, on another planet. I hear him say in a flat voice, in Italian: 'Recording of footsteps in fresh snow.'

He lowers the tennis-ball on the end of its rod and walks away downhill, his boots, when I listen for them, making a squeaky sound on the packed silence. I imagine his arrival among the villagers in the square, an utter stranger who has appeared overnight out of nowhere, in foreign garb and moving about with that amazing rod in his hand, like an Eskimo who has gone fishing on the ice and got somewhat lost. Struck silent, they follow him about. He is talking to himself, utterly absorbed in some world of his own.

It is the quality of his absorption that fascinates them, as it does me: a man involved in his own mystery, his own *mystère*, walking about a village he has never seen before, forming his own picture of it, his own map; getting to know it, but through one sense only; recreating it in the intangible dimension of sound.

He goes into Alma's dim little bar and sits there in his hood, incommunicable among the drinkers and card-players like Death in an engraving. Then, without a word, he gets up with his rod and goes out again.

He pauses to record the trickle of a fountain, birds in a bare tree, the scrape of shovels where men are clearing snow, children's voices, turkey gobblers, dogs barking far off then close. Later, when we listen to them, the whole village will be here. These are the sounds of my walk. They will be added, seamlessly, as if they belonged to a single experience, to the broken bits and pieces of the walk I am taking, since that, as we film it, is silent.

So we set out uphill. We begin filming with a shot of the bell tower at the top of my street, all gold in the early light, its two heavy bells in silhouette against an expanse of brilliant blue.

The tripod is set up. Bob tries one angle, then another, then a third. He is hard to please.

Yes, this is it.

Richard places me off to the right and I have a practice walk-through while the camera follows me.

'That's fine. Let's go.'

I go back to my starting place and walk again. This time the camera is whirring.

'Cut!'

I have walked ten feet from nowhere to nowhere.

We pack up. Adriano shoulders the heavy tripod, Bob has the camera. We move perhaps ten feet. Then Richard decides he would like a shot of a loquat tree I have pointed out while we were standing waiting for the last shot to be prepared. It is covered with snow. Once again the tripod is set up, shifted, set up in a new place. I move away into a patch of sunlight (the shot is to be made without me) and jog on the spot to keep warm. Bob makes his quiet, keen decisions, always without fuss, but several times changing things in consultation with Adriano till they get it right.

Bob has what my mother would have called 'a face like a map of Ireland', but is, in fact, New York Jewish. He wears woollen mittens that leave his fingers free and a dark overcoat. With his navy beret and the heavy black camera on his arm he looks like a Christian Brother turned I.R.A. gunman.

Richard, who never feels the cold, is bare-headed, gloveless, and wears a greenish leather bum-freezer and sneakers with emerald-green tabs and scarlet laces. He carries a still camera, turning off at moments to take shots, and a clip-board where he is keeping a record of what we film. He has never seen the village and has no idea what might be round the next corner. This walk is really taking place in his head, where he is putting it all together as it happens, creating his script.

Adriano, who is also bareheaded, keeps warm I suspect on his own intensity – you can see him being consumed with it – and by being so intent on what Bob is doing that he barely notices the world around him till it moves into frame.

He is a slight dark fellow of thirty-three or four, with hollow unshaven cheeks and very bright dark eyes, a fanatic. Bob tells us he speaks four languages, but since he seldom speaks at all it doesn't show. On a lace around his neck is the light-meter. He wears it like an amulet. He belongs to the same secular order as Alex and Bob – the order of those who submit themselves utterly to the machines they use, which they tend, attend to, push to the limit, but always with a respect that recognises in these objects both a finely-tuned power and the limitations that belong to their nature. Without these machines they would have nothing to do.

It is the ease with which they accept this as a condition of their own talent that I find so attractive. It makes them, for all their strictness and dedication, oddly without ego or that nervous anxiety that goes with arts where everything depends on the man and what *he* can do.

'Right,' says Bob at last, taking his eye from the lens and hoisting the camera on to his shoulder.

'Did you get the snow on the rails?' Richard asks.

'Yes. And the steps leading up to that little doorway. And the pink broom.'

'Great.'

Richard notes it all down. We move away downhill.

'You're on a sort of a walk around the village,' he tells me. 'We'll work out later where you're going. Maybe just walking for its own sake.'

'Hey,' Bob shouts.

Outside a house at the next corner a little fire is burning under an elbow of exposed water-pipe: three stove lengths of olivewood above a bed of ashes, making heat-waves but no smoke. Bob, shouldering the camera, gets down on his knees before it.

'Great,' Richard says. 'That's great. We'll just have you walk down the street towards it. Go back a bit. No, further. Further.' I wait, while Bob, still bearing the camera, tries positions, sometimes kneeling, sometimes sprawling in the ice.

We have begun to attract attention. Through a tiny window in the wall above the fire, a woman in black looks out. She has a cheesy unlined face but is very old. Her head is in a black scarf. She looks alarmed. What are we doing? She calls someone in the room behind, and a man in braces comes down. He is astonished to find Bob, the I.R.A. gunman, kneeling in his doorway as if worshipping the little fire, with this huge machine in his hands.

'It's good,' Bob shouts, ignoring the man. 'Let's try a walk-through.'

I begin to walk, self-consciously aware that faces have begun to appear now at other windows, over to my left.

'No, right on,' Richard directs, 'and round the corner. That's enough – you're out of frame.'

'It's good,' Bob shouts. 'Now we go.'

I get back to my mark, the camera begins to whirr. Richard gives me my call. I walk on down the street and am shot through heat-waves and little flames.

Bob struggles to his feet. 'That was great,' he says, grinning. 'I got a woman looking out of a grate.'

We go on, and at the bottom of the street come upon two small boys, one six or seven, the other a little older, dragging the kind of yellow plastic sacks that peat moss comes in. They are climbing the steep little street to a place where they can start a slide. They wear red woollen caps, red sweaters, blue track-suits. Brothers.

Richard is enormously excited.

'Hey, you kids,' he yells, forgetting for a moment that they are Italian, 'you want to be in our film? Ask them,' he tells Adriano. 'Tell them they can be in the film.'

The boys stand there in the snow, trailing their yellow sacks.

What we are about to set up is complicated. The younger boy is to go up a bank to the left, where he will be out of sight behind the remains of a ruined tower, and slide in, on cue, over a low stone wall. He will drop almost at my feet as I come uphill. (I am now, of course, moving around the village in a contrary direction, but that is neither here nor there. We are creating our own topography. The real village is dissolving, becoming imaginary, as my walk goes deeper into the world of fiction.) At the same time, the older boy will start sliding down the street itself, and pass me a moment later on my right.

Adriano asks the boys their names. The younger one is Michele, the older Fabio. We position ourselves for a walk-through as Bob sets up his shot. I go out of sight round the corner below. Michele climbs his bank. Fabio is flat on his stomach about ten metres up the road. Adriano calls the cues. '*Pronto*? – Michele! David! Fabio!'

Michele misses his cue. He is dreaming, or perhaps he is too far off round his corner to hear.

'Michele,' Adriano shouts as if he had known this kid all his life. 'What are you *doing*? When I shout *Michele* you *go*.'

The boy stands holding his yellow sack, solemn, crestfallen. Adriano explains once again the order of the shot. We try it and carry the whole action through; but this time Michele comes too soon. Perhaps he is too young for all this.

'Let's do the take,' Bob says. 'Tell him again.'

'Listen, Michele,' Adriano warns the boy, 'you better watch out. You get it right this time, eh, or you're out of the film.'

The boy climbs the bank again, looking determined. We all take our positions – go, go, go – and this time it's perfect. Michele comes rushing over the wall to my right, in a flurry of fresh snow, utterly surprising me. I barely have time to recover before Fabio is speeding down the street so fast that I have to step out of his path. I look back laughing as I trudge uphill.

'Cut!'

The boys are eager to know if they did well. Adriano assures them that he can get them both a contract at Cinecittà, but makes the conditions sound so much like hard work that they decide they'd rather stick to real life.

It is freezing now. We have been out for over an hour. This is the dark side of the village, away from the sun, though Bob assures us the light is just beautiful. The temperature is eight or nine degrees below and falling. We do not know it yet but this is to be the coldest day of the century. My feet are dead, and I have a sharp pain between the shoulder-blades from holding my neck so stiff. We go on down to the main square. (No sign of Alex, my double in the world of sound, the Eskimo space-walker.) Bob sets up to take a shot of me walking up the ramp towards the castle, mostly because at this moment the light is so good; is falling so nicely on the snow-covered railings of the ramp, but especially on two wordless traffic signs, one red, the other a brilliant blue.

Once again the geography of my walk puzzles me. But not to worry. The traffic signs have intervened to point directions. So I walk slowly up the ramp, then back again; then up, then back; while men come out of the bars on opposite sides of the square to watch. At last, when all is ready and Adriano has applied his light-meter to every significant object along the way, I set out under thirty or forty pairs of eyes, past the frost-covered rails and the door of the Tabacchi, and am quickly out of frame.

Noon. While Bob and Adriano, at the highest point of the village, take long-shots of chimneys across tiled roofs, Richard and I run back to the square to buy fish from the travelling fishmonger, who has somehow made it up from the coast. We have heard him shouting his wares through a megaphone – squid, prawns, three kinds of fish – and find his wagon drawn up under Alma's bare wistaria. We buy a kilo of squid and a kilo of crustaceans that look like big centipedes but are called 'cicadas'. The fishmonger explains that he usually gets them here alive, but today they are deep-frozen. (This is a joke?) He shows me the icicles hanging from the wooden trays that are stacked three deep in the back of his van.

It is twelve thirty by the time we find Alex and make our way to Alma's bar. We are all frozen, famished and in need of warming drinks.

We have been out for more than three hours. In that time, in my film life, I have walked thirty feet.

Over our hasty meal of dry bread with good Tuscan salami, we discuss our next moves. Bob would like to shoot my feet passing an iron wheel he has discovered, half-buried in the snow. Richard considers shooting me in the post office, or at Trento's, to create a reason for my walk. Meanwhile we are joined by the resident simpleton at Alma's, who wants us to shoot *him*, or his house, where the snow he assures us is wonderful.

He is called Bernardo. No more than five feet high, cross-eyed and always half-pissed, he wears a fur cap, a zipped-up blouson, and from now on will follow us all over the village, not speaking but reminding us with his presence, and the aggrieved look of a sulky child, that we are rejecting him.

We go out to find Bob's wheel. It's no go. The light has changed.

Things are changing fast now. A big yellow snow-plough has appeared and has already cleared the lower end of the village, leaving the streets there a dirty grey wash. Richard decides on a nice shot into a traffic mirror, in which the camera sees my reflection approaching with the snow-plough behind, then slips down to catch the real me in another perspective, climbing the slope towards the square. It takes Bob a little time to set this up. We do a quick walk-through then shoot it, and try another complicated shot beginning with a poster in bright colours advertising a tractor, then showing the snow-plough in motion as I pass it. We have to repeat the sequence several times before we get it right, and each time, on cue, though in fact it is engaged on its own business, the snow-plough backs and covers the same piece of street, as if obeying Richard's call of 'Again!', 'Cut!', 'Again!' And all the time Bernardo, the aggrieved child, stands sulking, just out of frame.

We make our way back towards the house. So my walk is circular after all, I *do* get home.

Sunlight now is flooding the archway that supports one half of my house, throwing all the rough paving-stones into relief and picking out all the rungs of the two olive-ladders that rest in swings under the tunnelled roof. I go into the little courtyard at the back, and we begin a sequence in which I collect three or four short logs from the woodpile, pass Bob on the left, and he follows me down through the archway, under the ladders, into light. Bernardo has got tired of all this for the moment and gone back to the bar, but he reappears when we start shooting what will be, I imagine, the beginning of my walk, a short sequence in which I appear out of the door of the house, bang it, and go dancing down the sunlit steps.

Richard is disappointed with me. The first time we shoot it I bang the door too hard, the key comes flying out, and instead of picking it up and going on – as in real life – I stop, waiting for him to call 'Cut', and we have to shoot the whole sequence again. Richard makes notes. Since we are still shooting silent, I will have to repeat this, later, while Alex records and then synchronises the sound.

Three thirty. Bob is worried about the light. It is changing again, beginning to be pink as the sun falls now over the snowy fields. We want all this part of the film to be shot in the same light, even if we *are* shooting it backwards from morning to afternoon. So I go upstairs, and we shoot the opening of the film, which Richard, looking up at the front of the house, has just decided on.

It is early morning. The green shutters of my study are still closed in their patch of sunlit wall. The opening chords of a Beethoven adagio sound, and as the lovely this-otherworldly theme begins to unfold, I open the shutters – Ah snow! – and closing the inner windows again, stand there for a moment behind the glass, sipping coffee from a big white cup. As I move away the Beethoven fades and my work-day is to begin.

'Cut!'

But our own work-day now is almost over. Disaster is about to strike.

We are out again on the cold side of the village, high up near the castle, where the snow is still untrodden. Richard wants to shoot a short sequence with sound. I stand in a nice patch of snow about a foot deep, my back to a wall with an iron grill, behind me a view of cold, snow-covered hills broken by lines of scrub. The temperature is twelve below. As well as the camera set-up, we have to worry now about sound. Wire is threaded down my right trouser-leg and I am hitched up to Alex's sound-box. His tennis-ball, at the end of its rod, hangs just in front of me, out of frame. I am to talk.

'What do you want me to say?' I ask Richard. He makes suggestions.

I am eager to begin because I have been standing in this position now for nearly ten minutes. All sensation has gone from my left foot. If we don't start soon my teeth will chatter.

'OK, I know what to say,' I insist. 'Let's try it.'

We begin. It goes well. I am just getting into my stride when a kind of high squealing sound makes itself heard. It is as if some small creature were being tormented beyond endurance and was setting up an animal protest. I suspect my left foot, but it can't be that. It is the camera. Do these machines have an endurance point beyond which they can't be pushed?

'It may be just the cold,' Bob explains. He hugs the thing. I lift my left foot.

'If not?' Richard wonders anxiously.

'Ball-bearing. I'll have to take a look.'

So here is Bob now, in the relative warmth of my upstairs study, in intense communication with his 'instrument'.

With Adriano at hand he has taken the camera to pieces; the parts are laid out before him and Bob studies them. Richard calls me in to watch.

Richard, who loves machines, is fascinated to see the anatomy of the thing exposed like this and the loving skill and inward understanding with which Adriano and Bob regard it. This is a love affair. Then too there is Richard's feeling for Bob. He admires him enormously, but his feeling for Bob's patience and dedication, his commitment to the camera, has something to do as well with what men share who are for the moment a team; a kind of affection we have no name for – it is unique. And then beyond all that, something more.

All the pieces of the camera are disconnected now, but Bob still sees them as a unit, a working unit, and it is this double view of the thing that he is working with. This, I see, is how the film itself must exist for Richard. In showing me Bob and the camera he is showing me something of himself. Perhaps he is afraid that I have missed, this morning, the director's part in what we have been doing. I haven't, in fact, but it is true: the dedication of the technicians to their instruments, their adjustments and readjustments, their fine skill and patience, are visible in a way the director's are not.

But the camera is not just cold. It has given up. The day's shooting is over. Tonight we will make sound recordings; Richard will interview me. At five tomorrow, Alex and Adriano will drive to Rome and get another camera while Bob sets up his lights. We put Jimi Hendrix on the record-player and Richard prepares the squid, Japanese style, with cloves and red wine, while I stoke my stove against the freeze.

Friday, January 11

Early afternoon. After a morning spent recording 'wild sound', we are out in the village again. Adriano and Alex are back from Rome and we have a new camera. Bob wants to make some tidying-up shots of the piazza before we move indoors.

Since the streets have been cleared of snow and are now grey slush we can shoot only from knee-level. Bob sets up on the ramp leading up to the castle and will take a long shot of me entering the square by the fountain and going to the door of Trento's bar. The shot will start high up on the windows of Agatina's sitting-room, where the shutters are open showing pretty crocheted curtains, peacocks, and will then pan left to take in the sign of the Bar Hawaii and down to find me entering from the left. It will then pan right again as I move to the door.

We try a walk-through, and just as I get to the double-glass door, Signorina Natalina, all dressed up for a fashionable day on the Riviera, with paint an inch thick, a cigarette in her dirty hand with its chipped red nails, and a bit of ratty yellow fur at her neck, steps out as on to a stage, all brilliant smiles: she thinks we have filmed her. Two or three lounging youths snigger, ironically applaud, and call out: 'Hey, take Natalina! Get a film of Natalina.' She growls at them, makes a stabbing motion with her cigarette, then smiles again, apologises for their crudeness, and asks if her entrance was all right.

Natalina is a squat, powerful, ugly woman of seventy. She

changes costume two or three times a day, appearing in extraordinary creations of white or cream silk with all the accessories in emerald green or brown or scarlet, and goes from one heated place in the village to another – bank to post-office to bar – buttonholing people, usually young men, clutching at their forearms and beginning a conversation that circles crazily back on itself and consists, you soon discover, of half a dozen formulas endlessly repeated. She is mercilessly teased by all the males of the village from six to eighty-six, ignored by the women, and is always blowing her lips out in a grand huff.

There is a story, of course. Natalina is the only daughter of rich but respectable parents. During the war she went with a German officer, who was married and deserted her, and the village women as soon as the Germans left shaved her head. She has, since then, spent fifty years here, her story being repeated openly to each generation and to each new arrival astonished (as anyone must be) by the apparition, among the austere women of this village, of a bearded blonde truckdriver in the gilded finery of a brave defiance or the loopy fancy-dress of an increasingly pathetic fantasy. Natalina is one of the village clowns.

Anyway, she steps out now, all smiles, into the square, and I have to explain to her that it was just a walk-through. If she wants actually to appear she must go back inside and do it all over again. On signal.

Grumpy but eager to please, she agrees; but hasn't enough wit to grasp what is required of her. She keeps putting her head out of the door, calling 'When?', then stepping back to check her make-up, then stamping impatiently as she peers through the glass. Finally, after poking her head out for the seventh time, she loses interest – or perhaps she thinks we are simply teasing her.

She goes stamping off, but comes to a halt in front of the bank, about ten metres on, watching across her shoulder while we film the sequence. Bianca from the hardware store, and her fat daughter and grandchild, all in snowboots, have come along at just the right moment and go into the bar before me. Natalina is furious. She fumes off in her fashionable high heels, twitching her bit of fur.

Bob has now to take a still shot of the fountain, a cast-iron affair, bluish-grey, with a lion's head on each of its four faces and a ball and spike on top, the spout bearded today with coils of ice but beginning to drip. The shot will take a little time to set up because the road slopes steeply downward. The camera must be propped. Richard and I use the break to slip upstairs and see Agatina.

She has heard about the film, of course, and will have been watching from one of her windows. She offers us whisky, lays out biscuits, and then shows Richard her trick with the cats. Setting one of them down at her feet, she leans forward with her arms joined and urges it to jump. The cat, the deaf white one, looks distracted. She stamps her foot and urges again. Almost absently, but with marvellous ease, the cat leaves the ground, flies, clears Agatina's encircling arms, comes soundlessly to the kitchen floor and trots quickly away.

We are led off now on a tour of the house. We see beds with lacquered headpieces inlaid with mother-of-pearl, eighteenth-century commodes, cushion-covers, doilies, the long handmade pieces, all delicate lace, that hang between the curtains in public rooms. Agatina's parlour is full of old farmhouse copper-pots, kettles, ornamental moulds, together with trivets, three-legged footstools. It takes time to do justice to these things, and when we get downstairs the others are nowhere to be seen.

We find them in the bar. Bob now has the shot he has been eager for all along and which I, out of embarrassment, have tried to dissuade him from: Trento's in full action. Everyone is there, including Natalina and even Bernardo (who *has* got into the film at last). The tables are crowded. Trento, all proprietorial pride, stands moonfaced at the espresso machine. The windows at the back are open and flooded with light, giving the smoky space and its figures a ghostly look, as men slap down cards, old fellows grin and shake their walking-sticks at the camera, everyone steams and shouts.

Late afternoon: my working-room at the top of the house; but so changed that I scarcely recognise it. The furniture from one half of the room has been carried across the hall, and in its place stand gauze reflector-screens fixed to a frame with ordinary housepegs (mine) and three powerful lamps. Black wires trail away in all directions or are coiled in heaps. To save us from tripping they are fixed to the floor, every metre or so, with adhesive strips, and Adriano has cut several more in case they are needed. Pressed with a thumb to the edge of my desk, the doorframe, the walls, they hang in uneven lengths, all quite practical and within easy reach of a busy hand, but giving the room an out-of-season festive look. I am reminded of something oriental and it takes me a little time to recall what it is: Chinese or Japanese poems, trailing bannerlike from the branches of trees . . .

Alex is wrapping the lights in paper now, clear blue, that crackles like cellophane. The tripod is set up, the sound-box appears. Once again I am hooked up to it with a wire down the leg of my trousers. This is no longer my working-room, though the sense of its being mine, in all the solitude and austere discipline of the writer's existence, is just what we are trying to suggest. It is theirs – Bob's, Adriano's, Alex's – site of twentieth-century technologies that have long since superannuated paper and pen. I am squeezed into a corner, behind my typewriter behind my desk. Bob consults the lens, then steps forward to adjust the desk-lamp – not for my convenience but to make its light fall in a particular spot among my papers and to bring its elegant, conical shade into a more aesthetic relationship with my head. He checks this and makes a little clucking sound, then steps forward and drops the paper-support on the typewriter. It is catching glare. The windows behind me have the inner shutters open. Bright sunlight pours in. But the glow of the lamps is infinitely stronger.

Too quickly now we are finished, the film is in the can – or rather the fifty or so bits and pieces of it that will sit in a refrigerator in Milan for a time, and must then be developed, juxtaposed and assembled into a form.

I stand looking out across the landscape, in pretty much the same position as the one Richard has chosen for the opening of the film. A big red sun hangs over the hills, and the snowy fields, with patches of black scrub between, are glaucous with a sickly glow, a kind of greasy rose-pink. By tomorrow or the day after, the snow will be gone; the transformation will be reversed and become a story that some child in the village (one of our snow boys, perhaps, Fabio or Michele) will tie his life to across fifty years, as Baldo does the winter of '29. And we have it on film. You can see me taking a walk in it, from nowhere to nowhere. You can hear my footsteps, Alex's 'recording of footsteps in fresh snow'.

When I turn around again the room is being restored to normal. Adriano is tearing tapes off the wall with a sharp little *rip*. The lamps have been dismantled. Alex and Richard are easing a day-bed round the edge of the door-frame and back into the room. It is as if a life-film were being wound backwards. Soon the furniture will be in place and alone, my desk with the typewriter before me, I will begin to tap away in the silence –

Wednesday, January 9
When I got up this morning . . .

A Foot
in the Stream

[1]

Like most visitors I have been inoculated against it. Not only with the cholera-typhoid, polio and gamma globulin shots I have been advised to take, and the course of Paludrine I shall be following a month after I leave, but by all I have heard about the place, that mixture of legend, statistics and shocking hearsay that has made it the extreme human experience.

The fear of India. It comes in many forms. Fear of dirt, fear of illness, fear of people; fear of the unavoidable presence of misery; fear of a phenomenon so dense and plural that it might, in its teeming inclusiveness, swamp the soul and destroy our certainty that the world is there to be read but is also readable.

Air travel is a risky business. The days have long gone when we could depend on paying our money, climbing aboard in a clean safe place, and being wafted, six miles above the sore places of the earth, to another clean place further on.

Two years ago, on a flight from Australia, I found myself stranded in Bombay, and though the transfer from aircraft to five-star hotel was made as quickly and comfortably as possible, there was still a stretch of real earth to be crossed – in this case the outskirts of a city – and India imposed itself: light, colour, vegetation, a milling throng of pedestrians, bicycles, animals of every description. I could barely take it in, save in the broad sweep.

In lamplit shanties, in a haze of wood-smoke and dust, men

were tapping away at metal or scouring great copper dishes and pots. In other places, in the manner of all Third World countries, mysterious things were being done with car-tyres and inner-tubes; motor-bikes and cars were being worked on, all the parts laid out beside the road while mechanics in greasy overalls, or in shabby native dress, squatted or lay with their feet sticking out into the traffic. Naked children splashed in puddles. Pedlars spread their wares on a bit of carpet. Pigs rooted in garbage, cows wandered. It was all very dense and confusing.

Later, back at the airport, I had to run the gauntlet outside the old departure shed – more people standing, squatting, lying rolled in rags or blankets than I had ever seen in so tight a space. It was very nearly impossible to pick your way between them, and I trod, horrifyingly, on something soft. I thought it might be a hand.

I was waylaid just before the entrance by a mob of children, very slight and shrill and fiercely importunate. *Baksheesh, baksheesh*, they wailed, a dozen small hands tugging. I put my hand in my pocket, and in fumbling with the last of my Indian change dropped a shower of small coins on the pavement. They were immediately swept up. But the child who dived under my feet to retrieve them (he might have been seven) did not scurry off as I expected. He reappeared, holding the coins out to me on a grubby palm, and I saw that the little scene we were involved in had not been resolved by my clumsiness, merely suspended. We still had our roles to play out. There were dignities. This wasn't a grab-as-grab-can situation as I had thought. It had structure, a social shape that was in every sense to be *observed*.

I took back my coins, the children resumed their wailing; but I was hooked.

It is that little incident that has brought me back.

It is true of Europe as well, but one sees more than ever in a country as packed as this that space is one of the most oppressive forms of privilege.

Lutyens' design for New Delhi is grandly impressive, but the monumental layout, with its wide, tree-lined boulevards and infinite vistas – from palace, through triumphal arch into the mist of a winter dawn – makes shameless use of the rhetoric of space to proclaim a distant and unapproachable authority. Very appropriate no doubt to the Raj, but odd in a democratic republic. (The same is true of Washington, whose prototype, for all Jefferson's noble intentions, is imperial rather than republican Rome.)

Coming in from Old Delhi, where a single laneway not much more than shoulder wide has 600 goldsmiths' shops and the noise is deafening, I am very conscious of the regulation twelve feet of clipped green lawn between the tables in the Imperial Hotel garden and the subdued, cosmopolitan voices. This too is a pocket of the Raj. Dense foliage shuts us off from the roadway, and even the birds, wagtails and crows, are mannerly and few. Waiters in crisp white native dress, long coats belted with lime green and gold, their turbans of starched batiste, move about unobtrusively in sneakers. Quiet deals are being negotiated. Tourists are stepping back a moment to enjoy space and tranquillity, a time out of the real India.

Leaving Delhi just after dawn on the five-hour drive to Agra,

I feel almost disoriented by the emptiness of the avenues, the eerie absence, in this densely crowded country, of people. Patrician mansions, coolly classical, stand in immaculate gardens. In the bluish light children are making their way to school, all in clean school uniforms. Not far off a lone workman, who has been sweeping up, squats to piss. Others, wrapped in blankets against the cold, ride slowly past on bicycles to a place further on where some sort of work is in progress (the whole of Delhi is being recycled for the Asian Games). Great piles of earth have been flung up. Men are working with picks and shovels; women whose bright saris, green, orange, scarlet with gilt borders, go oddly with their status as the lowest form of manual labour, are removing the rubble in paniers which they balance lightly on their heads while ragged toddlers follow behind. Tents are pitched on the site and spill out across the wide grassy footpath. Cookfires are smoking, clothes have been spread for the sun.

Later, in a more distant suburb that is not tree-lined or grassy but baked red, the workers' encampment is more substantial. Mud walls have been raised to a height of eighteen inches and dun-coloured tents pitched over them. Soon, with tombs off in the distance among rocky outcrops that might be the fortifications of abandoned cities, we pass villages, also of mud. Everywhere in the early cold men are washing at pumps, in tanks, in canals or at village wells, standing in their loincloths and darkly gleaming as they pour water over their head and shoulders or stoop to wash their feet or rinse their clothes, which they lay out on bushes to dry.

We leave the city at last, but the stream of pedestrians does not diminish as one might expect. It thickens, moving in both directions at the side of the road: youths in smart Western dress, trousers and sweater, or a blazer with a starched open-necked shirt, others in skirts hooked up at the groin and an overshirt, faded but clean; others again in flowing pyjamas, some wearing turbans, others with what looks like a loose bandage round their head, many with their shoulders in tartan blankets, or with a scarf under the chin as if they were suffering from mumps; some barefoot, others in sandals or slippers; all moving at the same easy pace, in the stately, straight-backed style that makes walking look so good, so natural. There are no slouchers or shufflers here. They walk with purpose, and it is this that makes these crowds so odd to the Western eye. Where have they come from? Where are they going? They suggest some important rendezvous up ahead, a circus performance it might be, or a cricket match or political rally; just ahead or just behind. (But if it was behind we missed it, and if ahead we never arrive there.) Odd members of the crowd turn off into a village, or a whole line of women starts off across a field, or the throng swells round a flimsy settlement where food is being sold and passers-by can rest on benches or curl up on bare cots; but the stream never thins out. It might go on like this right across the country. The whole of India seems to be on the move between its borders, endlessly tramping, even when we are far out in the countryside.

People move four or five deep on either side of the main traffic, which consists of trucks, each with a metal canopy over the cabin painted with images of Ganesh or Shiva and draped with silver and gold tinsel (they look, as they approach, like fast-moving altars that have mown down a forest of Christmas trees), buses, carts drawn by yoked brahmahs with their horns painted sky-blue, lime green, yellow or by little white asses piled to four times their height with thatching, drays with enormous worn-down truck-tyres drawn by graceful slow-stepping camels, behind which the all-India transport drivers lean on their horns and blare.

Occasionally, at the side of the road, a casualty. One truck is tipped forward with both its front wheels removed; it has been brought to its knees. Another, further on, with its off-wheels missing, is an elephant on its side. This is not just fancy or 'a way of putting things'. One feels here that machines, in joining the animal forms of transport, have entered a single stream of creation that includes men, beasts, birds, insects, trees. The inclusiveness of the Indian, and specifically the Hindu view, subtly blurs in the mind as in the eye our usual categories.

This promiscuousness of India, its teeming plenitude, far from being oppressive, seems invigorating. It humbles but lifts the spirit. It seems immemorial, endless, indestructible. Things have been like this forever, and will go on like this, in defiance of every catastrophe, into a future too remote to contemplate. We will survive here, we humans, one species among many – that is what India promises. Even the economy, the real economy which is going on all about us and consists of millions of hands engaged in the smallest of tasks, even that, as I know from village life in Italy, is unshakeable, because the shocks that open great gaps in Wall Street are registered here as the merest hairline-cracks in a dried-mud wall. If this life is closer to primitive beginnings, it is also further off from the distant, the inconceivable end.

Going down into the streets of Jaipur, among the stalls, the shoppers, the hawkers with their wares laid out on the pavement; among the sellers of *pan* with all the paraphernalia of the ritual and a row of bright, heart-shaped leaves set out on a metal tray; among the roasters of peanuts with their coke stoves, the spice sellers, sweet sellers, schoolchildren, loungers, rickshaw-men waiting for fares, street-musicians in costume playing one-stringed fiddles, cows, dogs, camel-drays, I was amazed by the number of individual traders with nothing much for sale except a few trinkets or half a dozen pencils or lumps of quartz.

There is so much enterprise here. A little girl of not much more than eight is selling handkerchief-sized kites to her contemporaries outside a school, they in smart uniforms, she in rags. In front of the City Palace a boy of maybe six, carrying a shoe-brush and tube of cream, suddenly scuttles out of the shadows, dabs at my left boot and begins polishing. He is very persistent. He talks and talks and rubs away even as I walk, and won't be put off. He has set himself up with the brush and cream as capital and is making his way. He is utterly ragged, shoeless himself and very dirty; I can believe that he is one of the many here who live and sleep in the streets. But he has such energy, such tenacity and resourcefulness, that I can also imagine him surviving as the dusty little sparrows do. He seems indestructible.

He belongs to a group of four or five such waifs who huddle in the roots of a fig tree. One of his companions scurries out. He has a sack. He squats beside it, lays out his stock and begins work. Rolling a coin in his palm he makes it disappear, then reappear out of his mouth, his ear, his nostrils, out of the empty air.

He is a working model of the system itself. His hands move swiftly. Very neat and economical in his movements, he is an automaton, a coin-producing machine that just happens, since this is India, to have arms, eyes, fingers, ears, and a mouth that, when it is not regurgitating fifty-paise pieces, keeps up a continuous but incomprehensible patter. The aim, as in every capital venture, is to attract interest. The least flicker of it in a passer-by and a kind of contract will have been signed in which the display becomes a performance and the boy will have won the right to be paid.

So it goes on. These are not beggars, they are small-scale entrepreneurs of their own skill and readiness to serve. There are millions of them. All it needs is the response of another individual and these tiny actions will be gathered into the dense, shifting economy of the place, that passage of coins, goods, services from hand to hand that keeps a whole subcontinent honourably alive and moving from one day to the next.

Real beggars are few outside the big cities, and even they have something to offer: a mark of fate, the ability to whine effectively (piteously, formally, lyrically in the case of two urchins outside the Jaipur museum), or the capacity to strike up with the passer-by a relationship that immediately establishes obligation, but of an obscure kind that is all the more difficult to deny.

In the abandoned city of Fatepur Sikri I am approached by a very old bare-legged man with a white beard and a clean, loose-fitting turban. He has chosen me because I am the only person in the huge open square who is not occupied with a camera. He points to the top of the Victory Gate opposite. It is 146 feet high.

'If the sahib gives 100 rupees,' the old fellow offers, 'I will jump from the top and the sahib can take a nice photograph.'

'But I have no camera.'

The old boy lifts his shoulders and grins. 'Well sahib, give me two rupees then because I am such a very old man.'

He delivers this as if it were the punchline of a joke, and I laugh and give him the two rupees, but feel the joke would still work if I did not. Only then it would be his turn to laugh and walk away.

It is difficult to explain the sense of freedom I feel at being for a moment outside history as we conceive it.

A simple example. The swastika, which immediately evokes for us a set of responses that may range from anxiety, guilt, terror, through a perverse joy in the glamour of violence to moral despair at what we are all capable of, remains untouched here by 'the facts of history'. That complex of forces that for Europeans has the code name Auschwitz, and which for nearly four decades now has darkened our notion of our own possibilities, has no power here, because in the history of this place Auschwitz never happened.

India has its own forms of oppression (and the evil of untouchability is dark enough for any society to bear) but they are of another kind. To step out of our own culture for a time does not relieve us of history, or of the human nature that flows from it; but it does make history relative, and leaves us surrounded for a moment by 700 million souls who are innocent of what we know because the culture, the 'human nature' that produced it, is not theirs.

Looking out of the window at Agra I saw something fantastic: a whole line of men with lamps on their heads, five petrol lamps each, shining new, arranged in a three-foot high pyramid. The men walked in a straight line – there were seven in all – beside a canal. Later I saw the same men, or others, walking along beside the highway with all the lamps lighted.

They are the lamps that light village stalls. You look up, and there in the pitch darkness of India is a brilliant tray of apples or little yellow cakes, or a row of white-shirted salesmen sitting cross-legged on a bench covered with a snowy sheet.

The oddness of Indian headgear: I don't mean only the men with the lamps, or the women balancing two waterpots, one of terracotta, the other of bronze, or the children staggering under a papal crown made of dung-cakes, flat little cowpats arranged in circles to a height of three feet or more. I am thinking of the caps in every shape and colour, the toques, turbans, headcloths, and the improvised combinations like the black scarf tied over a pink tea cosy worn by the driver's boy on the bus, and the smart outfit of the man and wife in the seat behind me, two black ghosts; she completely obscured by a knitted balaclava, only her eyes showing, and the diamond in her nose, he in a red patent-leather flying-cap with a peak and earflaps lined with fur.

P.H. is a computer engineer from Ottawa who has been working here on an engineering project. 'After six months in this country,' he tells me reflectively, gazing out at a village scene, 'I have come to the conclusion that at any given moment one in every three Indian males' – there are approximately 300 million – 'has his hand on his crotch.'

Drivers often turn out to be more interesting than guides. My driver at Delhi said nothing while the guide was with us, but the moment she got down to take a scooter became almost voluble.

He is a mountain man from Kumouan, Jim Corbett country up near the Sino-Tibetan border, very small and soft-spoken, about fifty. He asks me where I come from and what I do. When I tell him I am a writer, he informs me in his incomprehensible English that he is fond of poetry and begins, as we hurtle through the Delhi traffic, to quote. I take it at first for something from one of the local epics, but recognise at last the Bard: 'Under the greenwood tree/Who loves to lie with me?'

Our driver at Fatepur Sikri was a Hindu, very refined, in a neat ginger suit, yellow shirt and tie, and with impeccably polished shoes. An ex-driver for the R.A.F. The guide on the other hand looked ill and seedy, in a thin jacket much-stained and glossy with wear, a collarless shirt, dusty downtrodden slipper and no socks. His name, he told us, was Gordon. He had studied at St John's College, Agra, graduating in 1958, and was an M.A. Sad, sick and suffering keenly from the cold, he kept manoeuvring us into positions where the view mightn't be so good but where he could at least linger a moment in the sun.

Mr G. is full of facts. When he hears I am an Australian he immediately rattles off the names of all the states and their capitals, including triumphantly, Hobart. The Taj, he informs us in a poetic moment, is 'a tear on the cheek of eternity'. His excellent English has an oddly old-fashioned quality. 'What line are you in, sir?' he asks at one stop, and when we come to the shrine of a Moslem saint that he cannot approach because he has failed this morning to take a bath (it was so extremely cold) he begs us 'not to take it ill'. After a good deal of talk about religion, and the remarkable ecumenism of the Emperor Akhbar (who hoped to reconcile Hindus, Moslems, Christians and Buddhists in a single faith, and whose capital at Fatepur embodies the vision in stone), Mr G. confesses that he is a Methodist. He and the driver tease one another, amiably at first, then with subdued hostility.

Mr G. explains that the peasants here are too uneducated to use a tractor: they believe their gods are in the fields and are afraid of breaking their heads with the blades. The driver winces. Also, the peasants cannot be taught to practise birth control, they are too stupid. 'And after all, sir, sexual pleasure is the poor man's only entertainment.' Mr G. has two children, twin boys, though he tells us sadly that an older girl died less than a year ago. The twins were a mistake that fate has now adjusted. The driver has five children, all in Delhi, all healthy and doing well, two of them with degrees.

Mr G. stares hopelessly out the window at peasants moving slowly behind yoked oxen, and sucks at a thin cigarette, though the driver has already made it plain that he objects. When we get out again he makes immediately for the sun.

He and the driver have a brief, sharp disagreement over a bird. It is clearly a kingfisher, as the driver says, but Mr G. insists it is a jay, and he continues to insist as if his account of the number of Akhbar's wives or the height of a tower depended for their credibility now on the name of the bird. The kingfisher keeps reappearing, flashing its turquoise wings in pools, among columns, to taunt him.

Even at the end the driver gets the better of him. In a little difficulty about fares and tips I fail to make clear how much each man is to get, and when Mr G. demands an adjudication lose my nerve. I abandon him to the driver's goodwill. He looks hurt. I have played just the part in Mr G.'s world that has been assigned to me. For all his Methodism and his M.A. he is always on the losing end of things, even here when he might have expected of fellow Christians some sort of solidarity against the heathen Hindu.

Poor Mr G. His sallow face and thin shoulders, his inability to approach the shrine, his lesser share, our odd course round the sights as we follow the sun – all this will stay with me longer, I suspect, than the wonders he has to show us, impressive as they undoubtedly are. He will always haunt the place, like his opposing spirit, the flashy, blue-winged kingfisher that would not, for all his naming and renaming of it, become a jay.

I don't think I have ever been in a place that is so morally or spiritually dangerous.

India is full of temptations for the westerner. The temptations to voyeurism for example, to look on all this through a plate-glass window (or camera lens), at a safe, air-conditioned distance, and to titillate the eye, as the Sunday magazines have instructed us, with colour, action, and misery in its most picturesque forms. The temptation to play god, and with a gesture that costs us the price of a Coca Cola congratulate ourselves on our compassion, our human kindness. The temptation to believe that we have understood what we have been confronted with, that the commonness of human nature, coupled with an extraordinary personal sensitivity, has revealed to us the meaning of gestures, actions, movements of the heart that are impenetrably foreign and mysterious. It would take a saint to avoid all these temptations and no one does; but it's as well to be aware of them and to remember that India is subtle. Any new occasion may spawn a temptation you have not yet taken account of.

I give two rupees to a young man in a dirty headcloth, but very bright and cheerful-looking, who is wheeling on a wooden cart a woman with neither fingers nor toes. The two rupees produce a look of astonishment as at a miracle. The young man lights up. The whites of his eyes and his white teeth appear. He opens his palms as before a divinity. I am invited to see myself as a kind of god, a fountainhead of miracles.

I turn away, embarrassed. Not only by the accident that has made me one of the gods, or by the man's gesture, which looks spontaneous but probably isn't, but by the number of factors in this encounter that I cannot hope to understand.

How far is this display of wonder a formal offering to my self-esteem? What is the relationship between this handsome, able-bodied youth and the woman? Is he her protector, or is she in fact being exploited by him and with what willingness on her part or under what compulsion?

These questions are unanswerable and they make all such occasions painful in the extreme. To walk on blindly as if no need existed, or as if all this were mere theatre, is to be in one moral predicament; to react puts you immediately in another. And of course to be concerned with moral predicaments at all is an indulgence, if all it involves is the desire to be in the right.

No element in the street scene here is so strange to Western eyes as the way animals, not all of them entirely tamed, move in and out of the lives of men.

We like animals in their place: lions in cages, cats and dogs at the fireside (replete with canned food and expensively packaged niblets in the shape of bones), bullocks out west or in plastic for the grill. Our exile from the Garden brought us absolute power over the rest of creation in exchange for a guilt we are free to feel or not as we please – on the whole a convenient bargain.

India seems never to have heard of this absolute distinction on which our superiority and power is based. Man and the beasts form a single stream. Cows roam freely in the streets and are fed but not eaten. (In the market at Jaipur I saw them feeding on pomegranates.) There are stray dogs everywhere, of a kind one never sees in Europe, lean creatures out of a mediaeval Apocalypse, the females with enormous teats; also hairy half-wild pigs, sometimes black, often brindled, with very pink naked-looking piglets. Goats wander in flocks, almost always without a herder. Most engaging of all are the squirrels, grey with a triple stripe down the back where they were stroked by Lord Krishna; and the ubiquitous, shamelessly playful, serious-sad and free-ranging monkeys.

In the main street of Jaipur, I glanced up at the elegant pink facade opposite, with its pepper-pot domes and pierced screens, and was astonished to see swift grey monkeys flying about above the heads of the pedestrians, swinging through the air from sill to parapet, from ledge to tower, and realised that on my side too they must be right above me, as indeed they were.

In the eighteenth-century Astronomy Park, the instruments of heavenly calculation are disposed like giant pieces in a game, or like modern geometric sculptures – a stairway sixty-five feet high, leading nowhere but permanently fixed on the Pole Star, a granite sun-dial, two sunken hemispheres, one the complement of the other, with marble head-rests beautifully inscribed where the star-gazer can rest his head on the name of Aldebaran and find the star itself immediately overhead. In that quiet place, among the giant discs and triangles and free-standing figures of the zodiac, monkeys lope about like stoop-shouldered scholars grown small and grey with thinking or with having looked down the wrong end of the evolutionary telescope. They settle and sit chin on hand, brooding.

The animals are everywhere, either as companions in labour or as beasts left free to wander in their own lives, but always as creatures who belong to a single creation that has not yet been culled and cowed and simplified in the interests of a dominant species. It is easy to see here how one might develop an attitude of non-violence towards the creatures out of a belief that the same spirit of energy plays up and down from the lowest forms of life to the most complex and refined.

My only remaining fear is of being bitten: by a rabid dog, I tell myself, or by a bat in the cave temples at Ellora, but really, I think, by India itself.

I have a dream in which I am moving through a garden full of cobwebs, like the white cobwebby frost that covered the whole landscape when we came in to land at Delhi in the early dawn. I wade through it, using my hands to open a path and avoiding the odd scorpion-like creatures, fat and orange-yellow, that hang in the webs, until my left hand is swathed in the stuff, a heavy white glove. I am almost through when one of the scorpions fastens on my right hand and stings, but without pain, in fact with a painless but paralysing sweetness; and I think of the shoeshine boy in the Tibetan market on Janpath who, while I am momentarily distracted, has put a dab of cream on my boot and suddenly throws up his hands exclaiming: 'But what is this, sahib? What is this I see?' So that once again I am involved in a drama, a relationship from which I cannot be extricated save by the offer, as always, of a propitiatory fee.

How much of what I see here do I really take in? Everything happens so fast, there is so much of it, and the language of human gesture is not universal.

At Agra we were shown artisans at work in a marble factory. In the yard outside, where great slabs were being unpacked from straw, half a dozen youths were skylarking about in a boisterous universal manner; but on the open verandah, where three others were at work gouging out designs with a chisel, shaping the semi-precious stones on a wheel to make leaf-and-flower motifs and painstakingly setting them, something occurred that I could not interpret and still can't.

One of the boys (he might have been fifteen), using a pair of tweezers and a live coal, was engaged in setting the stones in a white paste. Suddenly, as the factory owner turned away a moment, he gave us a wild look and held up four fingers in some sort of appeal. Another demand for rupees? It looked like more than that. In a more melodramatic situation it would quite clearly have been a sign that he was being held against his will, a desperate cry for rescue.

Nothing explained itself, we passed on. But I see that wordless gesture, four tense upthrust fingers and an open mouth, as an image of what I have failed to understand here, a message I am deaf to and have not received, an uncomfortable reminder of the million tiny events I have been present at that escaped my attention and which added together would make a wall of darkness in which what I have seen is the merest flash of chips in a mosaic, an eye, a hand, the fragment of a broken arch, the passage of a kingfisher's, a bluejay's wing.

The Kyogle Line

[1]

In July 1944, when train travel was still romantic, and hourly flights had not yet telescoped the distance between Brisbane and Sydney to a fifty-five minute interval of air-conditioned vistas across a tumble of slow-motion foam, we set out, my parents, my sister and I, on the first trip of my life – that is how I thought of it – that would take me over a border. We left from Kyogle Station, just a hundred yards from where we lived, on a line that was foreign from the moment you embarked on it, since it ran only south out of the state and had a gauge of four-foot-eight. Our own Queensland lines were three-foot-six and started from Roma Street Station on the other side of the river.

I was familiar with all this business of gauges and lines from school, where our complicated railway system, and its origins in the jealously guarded sovereignty of our separate states, was part of our lessons and of local lore, but also because, for all the years of my later childhood, I had seen transports pass our house ferrying troops across the city from one station to the other, on their way to Townsville and the far north. We lived in a strip of no-man's-land between lines; or, so far as the thousands of Allied troops were concerned, between safe, cosmopolitan Sydney and the beginning, at Roma Street, of their passage to the war.

Our own journey was for a two weeks' stay at the Balfour Hotel at the corner of King and Elizabeth Streets, Sydney. The owner was an old mate of my father's, which is why, in wartime, with all hotel rooms occupied, we had this rare chance of accommodation. Train bookings too were hard to come by. We would sit up for sixteen hours straight – maybe more, since the line was used for troop movements. I was delighted. It meant I could stay up all night. Staying awake past midnight was also, in its way, a border to be crossed.

I had been many times to see people off on the 'First Division', and loved the old-fashioned railway compartments with their foliated iron racks for luggage, their polished woodwork, the spotty black-and-white pictures of Nambucca Heads or the Warrumbungles, and the heavy brocade that covered the seats and was hooked in swags at the windows. When we arrived to claim our seats, people were already crammed into the corridor, some of them preparing to stand all the way. There were soldiers in winter uniform going on leave with long khaki packs, pairs of gum-chewing girls with bangles and pompadours, women with small kids already snotty or smelly with wet pants, serious men in felt hats and double-breasted suits. The afternoon as we left was dry and windy, but hot in the compartment. It was still officially winter. When the sun went down it would be cold.

My mother would spend the journey knitting. She was, at that time, engaged in making dressing-gowns, always of the same pattern and in the same mulberry-coloured nine-ply, for almost everyone she knew. There was rationing, but no coupons were needed for wool. I had been taught to knit at school and my mother let me do the belts – I had already made nine or ten of them – but was waiting because I didn't want to miss the border and the view.

What I was hungry for was some proof that the world was as varied as I wanted it to be; that somewhere, on the far side of what I knew, difference began, and that the point could be clearly recognised.

The view did change, and frequently, but not suddenly or sharply enough. It was a matter of geological forms I couldn't read, new variants of eucalypt and pine. The journey from this point of view was a failure, though I wouldn't admit it. I stayed excited and let my own vivid expectations colour the scene. Besides, it wasn't a fair test. We had barely passed the border when it was dark. It did get perceptibly colder. But was that a crossing into a new climate zone or just the ordinary change from day to night? The train rocked and sped, then jolted and stopped for interminable periods in a ring-barked nowhere; then jerked and clashed and started up again. We saw lights away in the darkness, isolated farmhouses or settlements suggesting that some of the space we were passing through was inhabited. We got grimy with smuts.

My mother knitted, even after the lights were lowered and other people had curled up under blankets. I too kept wide awake. I was afraid, as always, of missing something – the one thing that might happen or appear, that was the thing I was intended not to miss. If I did, a whole area of my life would be closed to me for ever.

So I was still awake, not long after midnight, when we pulled into Coff's Harbour and the train stopped to let people get off and walk for a bit, or buy tea at the refreshment room.

'Can *we*?' I pleaded. 'Wouldn't you like a nice cup of tea, Mummy? I could get it.'

My mother looked doubtful.

'It wouldn't do any harm,' my father said, 'to have a bit of a stretch.'

'I need to go to the lav,' I threw in, just to clinch the thing. It had been difficult to make your way through standing bodies and over sleeping ones to the cubicles at either end of the carriage. The last time we went we had had to step over a couple, one of them a soldier, who were doing something under a blanket. My father, who was modest, had been shocked.

'Come on then.' We climbed down.

It was a clear cold night and felt excitingly different, fresher than I had ever known, with a clean smell of dark bushland sweeping away under stars to the escarpments of the Great Divide. People, some of them in dressing-gowns and carrying thermos flasks, were bustling along the platform. The train hissed and clanged. It was noisy; but the noise rose straight up into the starry night as if the air here were thinner, offered no resistance. It felt sharp in your lungs.

We passed a smoky waiting-room where soldiers were sprawled in their greatcoats, some on benches, others on the floor, their rifles in stacks against the wall; then the refreshment room with its crowded bar. It was a long walk to the Men's, all the length of the platform. I had never been out after midnight, and I expected it to be stranger. It *was* strange but not strange enough. In some ways the most different thing of all was to be taking a walk like this with my father.

We were shy of one another. He had always worked long hours, and like most children in those days I spent my time on the edge of my mother's world, always half-excluded but half-involved as well. My father's world was foreign to me. He disappeared into it at six o'clock, before my sister and I were up, and came back again at tea-time, not long before we were packed off to bed. If we went down under-the-house on Saturdays to watch him work, with a stub of indelible pencil behind his ear, as some men wear cigarettes, it was to enter a world of silence there that belonged to his deep communication with measurements, and tools, and dove-tail joints that cast us back on our own capacity for invention.

He was not much of a talker, our father. He seldom told us things unless we asked. Then he would answer our questions too carefully, as if he feared, with his own lack of schooling, that he might lead us wrong. And he never told stories, as our mother did, of his family and youth. His family were there to be seen, and however strange they might be in fact, did not lend themselves to fairytale. My father had gone out to work at twelve. If he never spoke of his youth it was, perhaps, because he had never had one, or because its joys and sorrows were of a kind we could not be expected to understand. There was no grand house to remember, as my mother remembered New Cross; no favourite maids; no vision of parents sweeping into the nursery to say goodnight in all the ballroom finery of leg o'mutton sleeves and pearl combs and shirt-fronts stiff as boards. His people were utterly ordinary. The fact that they were also *not* Australian, that they ate garlic and oil, smelled different, and spoke no English, was less important than that they had always been there and had to be taken as they were. Our father himself was as Australian as anyone could be – except for the name. He had made himself so. He had played football for the State, and was one of the toughest welter-weights of his day, greatly admired for his fairness and skill by an entire generation.

But all this seemed accidental in him. A teetotaller and non-smoker, very quiet in manner, fastidiously modest, he had an inner life that was not declared. He had educated himself in the things that most interested him, but his way of going about them was his own; he had worked the rules out for himself. He suffered from never having been properly schooled, and must, I see now, have hidden deep hurts and humiliations under his studied calm. The best he could do with me was to make me elaborate playthings – box-kites, a three-foot yacht – and, for our backyard, a magnificent set of swings. My extravagance, high-strung fantasies, which my mother tended to encourage, intimidated him. He would have preferred me to become, as he had, a more conventional type. He felt excluded by my attachment to books.

So this walk together was in all ways unusual, not just because we were taking it at midnight in New South Wales.

We walked in silence, but with a strong sense, on my part at least, of our being together and at one. I liked my father. I wished he would talk to me and tell me things. I didn't know him. He puzzled me, as it puzzled me too that my mother, who was so down on our speaking or acting 'Australian', should be so fond of these things as they appeared, in their gentler form, in him. She had made, in his case, a unique dispensation.

On our way back from the Men's we found ourselves approaching a place where the crowd, which was generally very mobile, had stilled, forming a bunch round one of the goods wagons.

'What is it?' I wanted to know.

'What is it?' my father asked another fellow when we got close. We couldn't see anything.

'Nips,' the man told us. 'Bloody Nips. They got three Jap P.O.W.'s in there.'

I expected my father to move away then, to move me on. If he does, I thought, I'll get lost. I wanted to see them.

But my father stood, and we worked our way into the centre of the crowd; and as people stepped away out of it we were drawn to the front, till we stood staring in through the door of a truck.

It was too big to be thought of as a cage, but was a cage, just the same. I thought of the circus wagons that sometimes came and camped in the little park beside South Brisbane Station, or on the waste ground under Grey Street Bridge.

There was no straw, no animal smell. The three Japs, in a group, if not actually chained then at least huddled, were difficult to make out in the half-dark. But looking in at them was like looking in from our own minds, our own lives, on another species. The vision imposed silence on the crowd. Only when they broke the spell by moving away did they mutter formulas, 'Bloody Japs,' or 'The bastards', that were meant to express what was inexpressible, the vast gap of darkness they felt existed here – a distance between people that had nothing to do with actual space, or the fact that you were breathing, out here in the still night of Australia, the same air. The experience was an isolating one. The moment you stepped out of the crowd and the shared sense of being part of it, you were alone.

My father felt it. As we walked away he was deeply silent. Our moment together was over. What was it that touched him? Was he thinking of a night, three years before, when the Commonwealth Police had arrested his father as an enemy alien?

My grandfather came to Brisbane from Lebanon in the 1880s; though in those days of course, when Australia was still unfederated, a parcel of rival states, Lebanon had no existence except in the mind of a few patriots. It was part of greater Syria; itself then a province of the great, sick Empire of the Turks. My grandfather had fled his homeland in the wake of a decade of massacres. Like other Lebanese Christians, he had sorrowfully turned his back on the Old Country and started life all over again in the New World.

His choice of Australia was an arbitrary one. No one knows why he made it. He might equally have gone to Boston or to Sao Paolo in Brazil. But the choice, once made, was binding. My father and the rest of us were Australians now. That was that. After Federation, in the purely notional view of these things that was practised by the immigration authorities, greater Syria (as opposed to Egypt and Turkey proper) was declared white – but only the Christian inhabitants of it, a set of official decisions, in the matter of boundary and distinction, that it was better not to question. My father's right to be an Australian, like any Scotsman's for example, was guaranteed by this purely notional view – that is, officially. The rest he had to establish for himself; most often with his fists. But my grandfather, by failing to get himself naturalised, remained an alien. At first a Syrian, later a Lebanese. And when Lebanon, as a dependency of France, declared for Vichy rather than the Free French, he became an enemy as well.

He was too old, at more than eighty, to be much concerned by any of this, and did not understand perhaps how a political decision made on the other side of the world had changed his status, after so long, on this one. He took the bag my aunts packed for him and went. It was my father who was, in his quiet way – what? – shaken, angered, disillusioned?

The authorities – that is, the decent local representatives – soon recognised the absurdity of the thing and my grandfather was released: on personal grounds. My father never told us how he had managed it, or what happened, what he *felt*, when he went to fetch his father home. If it changed anything for him, the colour of his own history for example, he did not reveal it. It was just another of the things he kept to himself and buried. Like the language. He must, I understood later, have grown up speaking Arabic as well as he spoke Australian; his parents spoke little else. But I never heard him utter a word of it or give any indication that he understood. It went on as a whole layer of his experience, of his understanding and feeling for things, of alternative being, that could never be expressed. It too was part of the shyness between us.

We got my mother her nice cup of tea, and five minutes later, in a great bustle of latecomers and shouts and whistles, the train started up again and moved deeper into New South Wales. But I thought of it now as changed. Included in its string of lighted carriages, along with the sleeping soldiers and their packs and slouch-hats with sunbursts on the turn-up, the girls with their smeared lipstick and a wad of gum hardening now under a rim of the carriage-work, the kids blowing snotty bubbles, the men in business suits, was that darker wagon with the Japs.

Their presence imposed silence. That had been the first reaction. But what it provoked immediately after was some sort of inner argument or dialogue that was in a language I couldn't catch. It had the rhythm of the train wheels over those foreign four-foot-eight inch rails – a different sound from the one our own trains made – and it went on even when the train stalled and waited, and long after we had come to Sydney and the end of our trip. It was, to me, as if I had all the time been on a different train from the one I thought. Which would take more than the sixteen hours the timetable announced and bring me at last to a different, unnameable destination.